TOMMY'S TEETH

TOMMY'S TEETH

And Other Tales

CLAIRE L. FISHBACK

ISBN: 978-1-970121-16-2 (Paperback)
ISBN: 978-1-970121-15-5 (eBook)

This is a work of fiction. Any references to historical events, real people, or real places are used fictitiously. Names, characters, and places are products of the author's imagination.

Cover Art by Claire L. Fishback
Book Cover Design by Steven Novak
Printed in the United States of America.
First edition. November 2023.

Dark Doorways Press
c/o Because Books, Ltd.
9878 W. Belleview Ave. Ste. 2322
Denver, CO 80123
DarkDoorwaysPress.com
info@darkdoorwayspress.com

Also by Claire L. Fishback

Short Story Collections:

Lump: A Collection of Short Stories

The Doll Room and Other Stories

Origin Codex Series:

The Blood of Seven (Book 1)

The Gorging of Souls (Book 2)

For Joannie and Robert

Contents

Introduction   xi

The Tumor of the East Wing   1
Bad News Bear   7
Doppelvision   9
Alone   29
The One You Feed   33
The Strangel   59
Hurry Scurry   63
Perfectly Safe   65
Tommy's Teeth   81
Amelia's Monster Part 1: Secrets and All   97
Amelia's Monster Part 2: Scars and All   109
Amelia's Monster Part 3: Secrets and Scars   141
Family Plot   149
Hiccups   177
Love At First Sit   181
In Sickness and In Swine   191
Bone Curse   211
The Scent of Blood   221
Dwelling   227

Acknowledgments   235
About the Author   237
Want Free Stories?   239

Introduction

This collection of stories started as a way to keep my fingers in the proverbial fiction pie and quickly turned into what I believe is a collection of highly unusual stories, each one weirder than the last.

Every one of these stories is near and dear to me. They reflect who I was at the time of writing them—how I was feeling, what was going on in my life, fears, anxieties, even the joyous parts, even love.

You see, in March 2022, I started my own business on top of my day job and on top of my *need* to write fiction. Writing is my way of escaping the world, of being in control of things I can't control, and of exploring my own feelings, thoughts, and darknesses. When you're building a new business, there's a lot of stress, anxiety, and worry behind it. Not to mention my old friends Self-Doubt and Impostor Syndrome. Writing these stories brought me back to what I knew I could do and do well. It was a way to center myself in a time when there was a lot of unknown, unknow*ing*, and feelings of helplessness.

I didn't have time to devote to a novel, so I wrote short stories for my newsletter subscribers. The plan was simple: I would write one story per month starting March 2022, and at the end of a year or once I hit at least 50,000 words, I would publish the collection. I hit 50,000 words in August 2023, but had one more story I wanted to add. I wrote "Dwelling" the morning of September 22, 2023 before breakfast (not bragging...okay maybe bragging. It's not every day I can write 2,000+ words in around an hour and a half).

How did you come up with your amazing ideas, Claire?

I'm so glad you asked! Even the most prolific writers with the most insane imaginations need a little help from time to time. I have several prompt generators from books to card decks to runes. For every story in this collection, I used the Storymatic® prompt cards. Each month I pulled a card, added an image of it to my newsletter, and wrote the story. The prompts used appear under each story title.

Some of the stories are brand new ideas inspired by the prompts. Others were ideas I had written in my idea notebook that just fit so nicely with the prompt it seemed like fate to finally write them.

I feel like I have evolved and grown so much as a writer since penning the first short story in my first collection *Lump* back in 2006. My style has gone from grotesque and shocking to more of a weird and chilling angle. Stories to make you think and wonder. Sure, there's still a bit of grotesque and maybe a touch of shock in some of them, as is to be expected of horror.

I hope you enjoy reading these stories even more than I enjoyed writing them!

Claire L. Fishback
September 2023

For more short stories, visit horrorandmore-er.com and sign up for the newsletter, in which you get free short stories for almost every month and pictures of my beloved pittie mix, Kira (worth it just for those, trust me).

You'll also get a free eBook with a sampling of stories from my first two short story collections, *Lump: A Collection of Stories* and *The Doll Room and Other Stories*.

The Tumor of the East Wing

THE SMELL THAT BRINGS IT ALL BACK

The room smelled. There was nothing the house could do about it. She'd seen much in her years. That *room* had seen much.

So many had passed through the house's doors. So many had been in that room. Met their doom. The house could only watch. Lament. Creak her floorboards. Open and close her cupboards. Even slam a door or two if she tried extra hard. The house wished she could get rid of that room, but that room was a part of her.

Though the room was tucked away toward the back of the first floor, the people always found it. Made plans for it. Figured out how to use it.

That room.

That vile room.

It had its own history, just as the house had hers. The room's history, though, was sordid. Bloody. Terrible. It made the house's eaves shudder at the thought of what transpired therein.

She'd been ripped open, gutted, renovated. New floors.

New windows. A new roof once or twice. Polished, painted, primed to be sold for double the price bought. But that room remained. Always there. Mocking her. A cancerous part of her. A tumor in the east wing.

The room remained untouched year after year, decade after decade, for nearly a century now. The house didn't know why the people didn't do something about it. That room. That nasty room.

She was for sale again, the house. She'd been on the market for quite some time now. Her price had dropped severely, despite the latest round of cheap renovations. The people had high hopes. Those hopes were dashed.

Because of the room. Because of what happened *in* the room.

The fix-and-flippers didn't realize they couldn't put lipstick on this pig. That room being the pig of course. The house herself was beautiful. She thought she was anyway. The people always said so when they first came in. Her open floor plan, her foyer, her grand staircase. If she had a mouth, she would smile at the thought of how beautiful she was. How the people decorated her walls. Filled her spaces with their furnishings. How they made her into a home.

Then the room got hold of them.

If she had a mouth, she would sneer. The most she could do was close its door. But the room always opened it again.

She tried to save them. All the ones who went into that room. She tried to keep them away. The best she could do was make them believe that area was haunted. *That* never worked. Most people were intrigued by the doors closing on their own. The floorboards creaking. The footsteps she mimicked by lifting her subfloors just enough to cause a muted thumping.

The room prevailed.

"What should we do with this weird space?" one woman asked. Her belly bulged with child. The house wanted to drive her out, both of them. A happy couple in their first home. *She* was their first home.

The husband, hand on the wife's lower back, peered into the room's dark space. No windows in that room. Just a door. Just a bare lightbulb. Just the stench of what came before.

The house pushed at the room's door, but the room resisted. The door only twitched in its frame.

"It could be a good storage area," the husband said with a shrug.

"Or a craft room," the wife said. Her eyes lit up. Her face lit up. She clapped her hands. She moved fearlessly into the dark space. "If only there were more light." She tugged the string. The bare bulb lit, flashed, burst. She screamed.

It was her first scream, but not her last.

They weren't the house's first happy couple. There were many more. Some lasted longer than others. Some brought children...

The house didn't like to think of those families. Didn't want to forget the crayon drawings scribbled on her walls, but didn't want to remember, either.

Her price dropped again.

The house lamented.

The man and woman—not a couple; she could tell by

the way they interacted—viewed the house several times. They unlocked her front door and stepped inside.

"Has nice bones," the man said again. He'd said that the first time.

The woman mused, arms crossed, peering around.

"It would be a shame, really," he said. He grabbed the house's newel post and jostled it. He sighed. "But it would be more cost effective to knock it down and rebuild."

"The structural issues are too great not to," the woman said.

Knock her down. The two wanted to knock her down and rebuild. It would eliminate the room at long last...

The room slammed its own door. The man and the woman jumped at the sound. It was a violent sound. Aggressive. The room wanted them. It had been too long. The house closed and locked all the doors the two would need to pass through to get to the room.

But still, they went. Cautious. Careful. Calling out to what they suspected was an intruder or a squatter—she'd seen her share of those, too. The room dispatched them.

As with all the others, the man and the woman had the keys to unlock all the doors. A different key for each door. She had little time to stop them from going to that room.

Knock her down. It would kill her, but it would kill the room, too. She needed these two. This man and this woman.

They were at the last door. The one that would lead them to the last stretch of hallway where the room held its door. The man fumbled with the keys. The room slammed its door again. They looked at each other again. They let out nervous laughs.

"Is someone in there?" the man called. The room slammed its door in response.

"Wind?" the woman suggested.

The house unlocked the door before the man found the key. She opened the door and slammed it in his face.

She opened and closed the other doors in the hall: open close, open close. Slamming doors, cupboards, windows even. She did everything she could to keep them from stepping any closer to the room.

They backed away.

"Tear it down. Rebuild," the man said in a shaky voice.

"Yep," the woman agreed.

They left the house.

The room slammed its door over and over in agitated anger. The house breathed a sigh of relief, all of her doors creaking open at once.

They knocked her down a week later. No one else would succumb to the room. The room would not eat again.

The new house, painted yellow and bright on a street of drab old gray and dingy white houses, sat on the lot. If she could whistle a tune she would. The crew had completed her on schedule and under budget. It was a joyous time.

Her first family—a husband, wife, and three children—moved in a few weeks later. Smiles. Joy. Awe at her high ceilings, open floor plan, massive kitchen.

They scattered to explore her rooms and hallways and nooks and crannies.

The house kept an eye on the children while they chose their bedrooms.

But then, the man called out. "Honey?"

The wife, in the kitchen stroking the house's granite countertops, called back to him. "Yeah?"

"Come here, check out this weird little room."

The room already smelled.

Bad News Bear

Bad news is a large wild animal. No
    one wants to bear it, nor give it,
    nor hold it inside them. It has
    to be shared. The beast released
    upon any open ear—willing to
    listen or not.
Freeing it is a one-way ticket to no
    return. It's out there now.
    You're *that* person. The one
    people avoid. The bad news
    bear. A cancer among friends. A
    vampire sucking the energy
    from every room you enter.
Here comes trouble.
You try to hold it in, but misery
    loves company, and you are the
    loneliest motherfucker out
    there.

You clutch your child's cherished
> toy against your chest.
Medicine isn't working.
There's nothing they can do.
Any moment now.
Best prepare.
Say goodbye.
The beast pours out of you
> uncontrolled. It passes through
> them crumpling their faces,
> rounding their shoulders,
> doubling them over with its
> unbearable weight. It leaks out
> of their eyes and noses. It wails
> from their grief-stricken lips.
It is theirs, now, to carry. To let
> fester inside before handing off
> to others the way you did to
> them.
You feel relief in letting it go.
A sickening lift and shift of spirits.
A devastating movement inside.
A gross satisfaction that you no
> longer must bear it alone.

Doppelvision

TELEVISION IS BROADCASTING ACTUAL MEMORIES

Trevor fell asleep with the TV on every night. That was the reason why he started turning on the sleep timer setting on his TV. Because some nights, before the sleep timer idea, he woke up during those odd wee hours, a mild nausea tingeing the edges of his consciousness, wondering where he was, the TV blaring on some B movie with a large-breasted woman grinding on a muscle-bound businessman. Fake sex for a fake couple.

The blue light flickering added to his mild nausea. His confusion. Sometimes he had to really peer around the room to realize where he actually was.

His own living room, kicked back in the recliner, empty beer bottle on the side table next to an empty bowl previously full of popcorn.

Sometimes, waking up like this, seeing the women and men in the late-night B movies made him lonely. Once he got his bearings, the lone beer bottle and the empty bowl seemed like significant indicators of a life not lived.

Trevor sighed, brushed a few wayward popcorn crumbs from his shirt, and got up. He collected the emptiness of his life and shuffled to the kitchen, dropped the bottle into the recycling bin and the bowl into the sink. He stood there for a second, looking at his reflection in the kitchen window. How the low light from the oven hood made his face look not his own, but like some incomplete interpretation of himself. A half-finished drawing.

Beyond the glass, the back porch light sensed motion and flared to life. A fox froze in the light, a rabbit dangling from its jaws. It looked at him—made actual eye contact through the clear pane—then slinked off into the shadows.

That was the last time Trevor fell asleep in front of the TV without putting on the sleep timer. That was over a month ago.

It was November. Trevor's least favorite month, though he couldn't remember why. One time, on a date, a woman named Shirley had asked him. She asked him a lot of questions, as if she'd studied a book, *101 Questions to Ask on a First Date,* or maybe a book about how to be interesting on a first date.

Trevor answered most of the questions with little thought and little interest.

He hated cabbage because his mother used to make it all the time, and the smell of it would get on his clothes, and the kids at school called him Fart Boy, which they later shortened to FB. Then they forgot what the initials even stood for, but the name remained and Trevor never forgot.

His least favorite season was the winter because of the cold.

"Why don't you move somewhere warmer, then?" Shirley had asked.

Trevor shrugged. He didn't have an answer, other than moving sounded like a lot of work, and he'd built his life— or the shell of a life—here in Colorado.

She asked him what his least favorite month was. "I bet it's January, since you hate the cold."

By this time, everything about her annoyed him. Her fake orangey-red hair. Her chipped nail polish. He didn't like the way her lipstick looked in the low light of the restaurant, like her mouth was bleeding. Or maybe like her lips were rotting with black blood poisoning.

He vowed not to kiss her goodnight, no matter how much he needed to feel another human.

"My least favorite month is November." Trevor put his fork down and sipped his water.

"November?" Her voice raised to an irritating pitch with the question. The nasal quality of it grated against his eardrums. "November's my *favorite*. It's the start of the feasting season." She shoveled a bite of food into her mouth.

Trevor just shrugged and absently looked for the server to get the check. He wanted the date to end. Too many questions. She questioned every answer as if Trevor didn't know himself enough to answer correctly. She didn't really know how to make conversation and it was all so shallow. He craved a deeper connection.

Outside the restaurant, Trevor shoved his hands in his coat pockets.

"Well, goodnight," he said.

Shirley rolled her eyes. "Okay, night."

He could hear the irritated disdain in her voice. Could hear how she probably thought the date was a waste of her time. He felt the same way.

At least he'd gotten out of the house.

November reminded him of Shirley and her questions, but that wasn't the reason he hated it. She was right. November was the start of the feasting season. But who cares about a feasting season when there's no one to share it with? That's what he didn't say.

But that also wasn't the reason he hated November. There was some *other* other reason. Some feeling of dread that came with it. No matter how many times he tried to pin it down, he never could. He hated November because of something he couldn't remember.

That night, he set the sleep timer on his television, kicked back in his recliner, drank his one beer and ate his one bowl of popcorn. When both were empty—like his life—he set them on the side table and snuggled down into the cozy chair.

Trevor woke suddenly with that sick feeling of his semi-conscious mind coupled with the disorientation of not knowing where he was. The TV was still on, flickering its blue light all over the room. He must not have been asleep for long since it was still on.

He looked at the clock. It flashed 12:00. The power must've gone out. Would that reset the sleep timer?

He wasn't sure. But it must have.

The show playing on the screen wasn't the usual B movie he expected. It was an old home video showing a young family. No sound. Trevor closed the recliner and leaned forward.

The woman on the screen—it was his mom. But...not like she looked like today. A younger version. Dark hair, not snowy white. A slim waist. A beautiful smile. The mom he wanted to remember.

Trevor slid down to his knees and crawled forward. The boy. It was him. His little sister bounced out of the house, pigtails springing up and down with each step. Trevor touched the TV. His little sister—Sandy—had died when Trevor was only ten. She'd been seven.

Trevor realized his dad must be the one filming. He'd also died. He and Sandy, together in a car accident. It shook his mother to her core. It brought them closer. At least he thought it had.

He didn't remember his own grief, just his mother's. He didn't remember feeling sad about Sandy and his dad being gone. As if he were one life removed or watching it like a movie. Grief was weird like that, he supposed.

But something had happened...something Trevor couldn't remember. It drove a wedge between him and his mom and their close relationship drifted apart. He still saw her. Once a month when he drove out to the senior community where she'd settled and visited for as long as he could handle being around the elderly—two hours maximum.

Though the people living there weren't dying and their minds were still sharp and not addled with dementia, he just couldn't handle being around them. They were old, but they were living their lives. He was in his forties and hadn't lived at all.

The home movie flickered on the screen and ended. The television turned off, and darkness dropped around him like a final curtain.

Trevor jumped and clutched at the front of his shirt as if making sure his heart wouldn't leap out of his chest. A chilling tingle prickled his skin suddenly, as if someone were in the room with him, watching him through the impenetrable darkness. It shouldn't have been so dark. There should be light from the street coming in the windows, light from the kitchen, from the oven hood.

Maybe the whole block went out.

Trevor crab crawled backward until he hit the recliner, then climbed up onto it as if it were a lifeboat in this sea of black.

His eyes searched for the flashing red numbers of the clock, but he did not find them. He groped the side table for his phone, knocking the beer bottle off. It clattered onto the floor but didn't break. The popcorn bowl, however, didn't fare as well.

Trevor found his phone and swiped the screen, hoping for the flashlight app. Dead.

By now, his breath came bursting in and out of his nose. He took a deep and shuddering breath through his mouth.

"Hello?" he called out, flinching against the loudness of his own voice in this pitch darkness.

No one answered.

The silence in his dark home amplified every shift of fabric on his body. Every scrape of his skin against the worn upholstery on his chair. He swore every time he moved, something out there beyond the reach of his recliner also moved, as if timing its own movements with his to mask them.

The lamp came to life. The TV came back on, blaring and loud with noises of false sex.

Trevor shrieked and flung a protective hand in front of his face. He glared around the room with squinted eyes.

Beyond the lamplight, the front door was open.

The remaining hours of the night, Trevor slept in his bed for the first time in over a year. He didn't drink a beer. He didn't eat any popcorn—his favorite popcorn bowl having been effectively smashed the night before.

Trevor had closed the door and locked it, turned on every light, and searched the house with a baseball bat in hand. He even pulled out a step stool and peered into the attic crawl space, having seen a movie once about people hiding there and coming out to live off of people's food and live in their homes while they were out and about during the day.

All was well. If someone had been in the house, they'd left before the power came back on.

Now, snuggled into his bed, Trevor wondered if he should get a dog. Not only for protection, but for companionship. Maybe that's what his life was missing. A companion animal to take away some of the aloneness he felt all the time.

The emptiness.

He tossed over onto his side, so unused to sleeping flat like this, he wondered if he should get one of those adjustable beds. He closed his eyes and smiled. Maybe he should move his recliner up here.

A sound tugged Trevor from a slumber he thought he would never find. He felt around for the TV remote and only found an expanse of cool bed sheets. He sat up, disoriented.

Right. His room. He hadn't awoken in this place in so long, but the light coming in from the street lamp outside his house gave him just enough to recognize the furniture. He yawned and stretched.

Children's laughter filtered up from downstairs.

Trevor's ears perked. His heart raced in a sickening staccato. He slid his feet into a pair of slippers, pulled on the robe that had been draped over the footboard since the last time he slept up here. It had a dusty smell to it. He dropped it in the laundry hamper on his way to the hallway.

He went to the top of the stairs and listened.

Children's laughter again, but there were no children in his home. The sounds had a separated quality. Filtered through time and the speakers on his television. Trevor clumped down the stairs and sidled into the living room.

The TV showed a scene he remembered well. It was his

birthday. There was a piñata. The laughter came from a collection of friends gathered around, watching him swing a broomstick at the piñata.

It smashed open and candy spilled out.

Trevor watched as the other children clambered under the broken shell of the donkey-shaped party toy, gathering the candy into their grubby little hands like blind beggars after coins.

Trevor the Child—it was his twelfth birthday—peeled off the blindfold. There was one piece of candy left. The other kids had snatched the rest of it up and run off to play on Trevor's amazing swingset.

A small branch waved in front of the camera, as if the videographer had been hiding in the bushes. It had to be his mom behind the camera, though. His dad and Sandy were gone by then, smashed up in the family car on a back street on their way home from the grocery store.

Trevor the Child on the screen sat under the swaying piñata shell, weeping quietly. Real-Time Trevor knew what would happen next. His mom would put the camera down and come to his side, ask him what was wrong. Trevor the Child would cry about the candy. She would present him with an entire bag of his favorite candies, and she would tell him she put the shit stuff in the piñata and saved the best ones for him. The memory filled him with warmth. His mom always looked out for him.

Trevor's mom came on the screen. "Oh honey, what's wrong?"

Real-Time Trevor, crouched on his living room floor, leaned away from the screen.

If his mom was there next to him, comforting him, then who held the camera?

Several nights passed chronicling Trevor's life in scraps of memory. He enjoyed watching his life play out, often smiling at the screen, sitting on the floor too close to the TV. Watching his mom and himself live their lives. In the back of his mind, he tried not to wonder who held the camera.

He'd moved back onto the recliner and, tonight, after a week of waking up to these family videos, vowed to stay awake. Instead of beer, he brewed a pot of coffee.

At 3:33 a.m., the TV screen blitzed and buzzed, filled with static, and a new memory came on. Trevor lifted the remote to check the channel, but the TV didn't respond to any of the buttons he pushed. It didn't even turn off when he smashed the power button as hard as he could.

The years had jumped forward. Trevor was graduating from high school now. His mom adjusted his mortarboard and tie. She kissed him on the cheek.

The cameraman filmed from off to the side. They zoomed in on Trevor's face, which looked nervous.

Real-Time Trevor, sitting in the recliner, didn't remember how he felt that day. In fact, a lot of the memories the TV had shown him he only remembered just like this: like he'd watched them from behind a screen. He wondered if Sandy and his dad's death had done that to him. Somehow mentally scarred him forever so he wouldn't feel. Like his brain was protecting him from powerful emotions.

———————

Another few nights passed. Trevor on TV was off to college now. He didn't move into the dorms, but got a job that allowed him to afford a small townhome. Real-Time Trevor couldn't remember his roommate's name. He racked his brain trying to think of who this person was. He had to be someone Trevor knew, maybe was close to. Otherwise, why share a place?

Eventually he stopped trying to remember the kid's name and instead fixated on who was filming him. The person was outside the living room window.

———————

The following two nights held much of the same. The camera found College-Aged Trevor around campus in various locations, talking to groups of friends, to girls, and studying in the library. Real-Time Trevor watched these with rapt attention. He didn't remember much from college, and several nights the program showed him at parties smoking weed and drinking beer. Maybe that's why parts of his memory were like an outsider looking in. He must have lost them in drug- and alcohol-induced hazes.

The time stamp in the lower left corner said November 13, 1999, 3:07 a.m. Real-Time Trevor's mouth dried.

November.

Sitting on the floor in front of the TV, he took a deep

breath and watched the camera move from window to window, always keeping the viewer with College-Aged Trevor.

After the party, instead of the usual hiding-on-the-outskirts shots, the camera followed College-Aged Trevor as he stumbled off campus, alone. He stopped and pissed behind a trash can. The cameraman tripped, let out an *oof* sound.

College-Aged Trevor turned.

The camera ducked back into shadows. The liquid stream of College-Aged Trevor's piss spattering the sidewalk and the cameraman's breathing the only sounds for a few seconds. Then the urination sounds ceased, followed by a muted zipper.

"Who's there? Josh? Jacob?" College-Aged Trevor laughed. It was a nervous sound. "Come on, guys, stop fucking around." His words slurred. It sounded more like, "Con gyz. Stop fknround."

After twenty seconds, according to the date and time stamp in the lower corner, the camera peeked around the brick wall. College-Aged Trevor was on the ground on his back.

He laughed with his hands on his stomach. "I fell," he whispered to himself. He let out another laugh when he tried futilely to get up.

Real-Time Trevor let out a breath of a laugh himself and took a sip from his coffee cup.

The camera moved forward.

College-Aged Trevor had stopped laughing. A soft snore drifted into the camera's microphone.

Real-Time Trevor leaned forward, inching closer to the TV.

A hand—the cameraman's hand—came into frame and pushed and jostled College-Aged Trevor. He slept, deep into a drug and alcohol darkness.

The scene cut. Real-Time Trevor jumped with the sudden change, flinched and cringed away from the bright lights in this new scene.

College-Aged Trevor was tied to a chair in a sparse room lined with plastic. Real-Time Trevor's eyes widened.

The timestamp read: November 13, 1999, 3:33 a.m.

The camera must have been on a tripod, because the cameraman came into frame, his back to the lens. He pummeled Trevor with his fists over and over and over again.

Trevor didn't watch the entire scene. He covered his eyes. Hearing the sounds was enough to turn his stomach.

When the sounds stopped, Real-Time Trevor lowered his hands. College-Aged Trevor was almost unrecognizable.

The TV shut off. The night's viewing complete.

"Jesus Christ," Trevor muttered. It couldn't have been him in the video. If it had been, he'd be dead, he was sure of it. He'd be dead or, if not dead, mangled with scars and lumpy disfigurement. He wouldn't look like himself at all.

Shaking, Trevor rose to his feet, groaning when his knees protested, having been sitting on the floor for so long with them bent under him that way. He went to the kitchen and threw the remains of his coffee into the sink; he pulled a beer out of the fridge and downed it.

It was disturbing, watching someone beat him up like

that. But what did it all mean? Was this some sort of premonition thing? Was it a warning?

He returned to the living room and stood behind his favorite chair, staring at the dark screen.

The TV came back on. Trevor cried out and ducked behind the chair. When he realized the TV wasn't going to hurt him, he stood.

The screen showed the back of Trevor's house, porch light illuminating a fox frozen in the middle of the yard with a rabbit dangling from its jaws. Trevor's face peered from the kitchen window.

The scene blipped, zoomed out until a man-shaped silhouette came onto the screen.

Trevor lifted his hand and scratched his ear. The same thing happened with the figure on the TV.

Ice drizzled down Trevor's back.

He raised both arms out to the side.

The dark figure on the screen did the same.

He turned.

A red light flashed from the kitchen doorway. A figure shifted. Trevor backed around to the other side of the recliner.

"Get out of my house," Trevor shouted.

"It's been a long time," a thick male voice said. The words echoed on the TV behind Trevor. The red light turned off, so did the TV. Darkness filled the room. "Exactly twenty years."

Trevor consulted his watch. November 13, 2019, 3:33 a.m.

"Why did you film me all my life?" Trevor blurted.

The voice laughed. "I didn't."

Trevor pointed to the TV, even though, in the darkness, the man wouldn't see him.

"I saw. You filmed me my entire life. Why?"

"No, no," the voice said. "You misunderstand." The light clicked on.

Trevor clapped his hands over his mouth.

The face was his, but it also wasn't his. It was disfigured with scars. Lumps where bone healed poorly. Sunken eyes where occipital bones had been crushed. But Trevor could still see himself in that face. In those eyes.

And then he knew. It all came back.

The emptiness, the inability to remember the things the video showed him.

He'd first seen Trevor when the two of them were both so young. He'd followed Trevor his entire life, learning about him, who he was, what his personality was all about. He tried to become him off camera, but he never lived up to who this Trevor really was. He'd always been a shadow of him.

"It was me," Trevor said. "It was me all along. Filming —" He swallowed the dryness in his throat. "Filming *you*." He took a shaking breath. "*Me...filming you*."

"You should have made sure I was dead," Disfigured Trevor said, sitting now on the arm of the recliner.

Trevor looked at his hands where faint scars crisscrossed his knuckles. Scars from beating this man to a pulp.

"I still took over. I still became you, like I was meant to," Trevor said, squeezing his hands into fists.

Disfigured Trevor shook his head. "No, you didn't." He lifted the remote and pressed Play.

A montage of Trevor trying to be, well, *Trevor*, ensued.

And these memories he knew. He felt them as each one flashed across the screen.

His mom shouting at him, yelling that he wasn't her son. Was it drugs? Was it something she did? Trevor's failed attempts to explain, to use Sandy and Dad's deaths as reasons for his change, but those deaths had happened so long ago, even his mom said so.

His friends looking at him strangely before shuffling off. They stopped inviting him to things. First Josh, then Jacob, then the rest. He became an outcast.

That was when the emptiness seeped in. The emptiness of a life lived through the lens of a camera. The emptiness of being a shell. A shadow.

The montage continued. He left town, the state. Tried to make a new life out in the Rocky Mountains, but there was just something missing.

A quick succession of all the dates he'd been on. The inability to connect. Scenes of him at work even, failing to join in the conversations with work associates. They all seemed to disperse once he came on the scene, as if the stink of his emptiness preceded him.

Like they could tell he was what he was.

"I guess this is it, then?" Trevor said to Disfigured Trevor. "You're here to kill me, right? Take back your life?"

Death seemed like it would be a gracious release, having seen the years he'd been this Fake Trevor through a camera lens, as an outsider. He'd never belonged. He was foolish to think he ever would.

November 13th. That's why he hated November. It was the day he realized—though he had succeeded in his life's mission—he never actually *could* succeed. He was destined to fail.

His kind weren't supposed to succeed. They were meant to be feared, always on the outskirts, like something one sees in their peripheral vision, but when they turn to look, there's nothing there.

To succeed was, in fact, the ultimate failure. The biggest disappointment.

A tear dripped down Trevor's cheek. He looked at Disfigured Trevor's mangled face.

"What happens now?" Trevor asked.

Disfigured Trevor moved so fast, Trevor hardly registered the bat swinging, and when it connected with the side of his head and he fell over, unable to bring his hands up to catch himself, he understood everything. A smile tugged at the corners of his lips.

He'd never really wanted this life. He recalled the night he'd beaten Trevor to a pulp and left him for dead, he'd stumbled out of that room. He'd thrown up in the alley, and when the contents turned to foamy bile, he'd sobbed.

Without Trevor, he had no purpose.

He'd squandered his time with Trevor's life. Had he even tried?

"Wait, stop," Fake Trevor held up his hands, shielding his face. "You can have it back."

Disfigured Trevor scoffed. "Have what back?"

"Your life. Take it. But please, don't kill me." From between his trembling fingers, Fake Trevor watched Real Trevor consider.

"Why? You're pathetic. Your life is pathetic." He tightened his grip.

"But yours wasn't," Fake Trevor said. "You can... You can help me."

"The fuck I'd do that?"

"Because I have your face. The face your mother loves. The face your friends know."

"Knew. They aren't my friends anymore. You destroyed every friendship I ever had. Even after I came out of the coma and remembered who I was...they didn't know me. Not this—" He released one hand from the bat and motioned to his disfigurement.

"Please," Fake Trevor whispered. "Teach me to be you. I want to feel what it's really like to be you." Sobs racked his body. Snot dribbled from his nose. "All my life that's all I wanted. To feel what you were feeling. What made you laugh? What did you feel? Or-or-or when you cried? To feel your grief when Sandy—"

"Don't you dare say her name." Both hands gripped the bat again.

But Fake Trevor could see Real Trevor softening around the edges. Fake Trevor knew—from over a decade of watching this man—he could be forgiving.

"I can't teach you how to feel," Real Trevor said.

"I want someone to like me."

"Who?"

Fake Trevor met Real Trevor's eyes in their deep sockets of broken bone. "Mom." The word came out a squeak. "I want her to hug me like she used to hug you."

"Yeah?" Real Trevor paced a few paces away, turned around. "I'd like to feel that, too. But she doesn't know me anymore."

He raised his bat and struck Trevor in the temple.

The emptiness embraced him. The darkness pulled him into its depths.

When he woke again, he lay in a hospital bed, bandages around his face. His vision in his left eye was blurry. Someone sat in a chair in the corner.

"Finally," his own voice said. Real Trevor stood and came closer, sat on the edge of Trevor's bed and leaned in close. "I was wondering if maybe I went a little too far." He leaned back. "*Now* I can have my life back. Let me show you something." He peeled the bandages off Trevor's face. "Mom came to visit you." He lifted Trevor's head to pull the bandages off. "She saw you all bashed and battered." He finished removing the gauze and lifted a mirror.

The face that peered at Trevor in the reflection was a mushy mess of pulpy tissue stitched together with black sutures. It wasn't a face. Not anymore. Beady eyes peered out through flaps of puffy skin.

"I'll have my life back, fully recovered—well, not *fully* fully, given, you know, my scars—and *you* get to be a horrible monster who will never *ever* feel what it's like to be me." He leaned closer. "You'll never *feel* anything."

Trevor tried to speak, but the words wouldn't come out.

Real Trevor wadded up the bandages and left them on Trevor's chest so gently it was as if they weren't even there. He walked to the end of Trevor's bed and grabbed his foot, gave it a jiggle.

"It'll be a miraculous recovery. The scarring not as bad

as mom thought it would be. She'll be delighted I healed so quickly." He played "This Little Piggy" with all of Trevor's toes.

Trevor didn't feel a thing. In fact, he didn't feel the weight of the blankets, nor where they touched his skin. He tried to sit up, he tried to lift his hand, he tried to call for help.

Real Trevor paused in the doorway. "Good luck, Trevor."

The door closed on his malicious laugh.

Alone

FIRST NIGHT ALONE

I awake in a darkened room. The kind of dark that you can just make out the details from some faint light source. This light source is gray. Everything is gray.

The room is different from what my mind thinks it should look like. It can't resolve the missing details.

There should be posters on the walls. There should be a mirror surrounded by pictures of my friends and me having great times together at school events and that spring break trip we took together last year.

Where are all my lotions? Where's my makeup? Where's my favorite hairbrush that my grandma gave me, the silver one with all the filigree or whatever it's called on the back of it with the matching hand mirror?

I rise from a creaky bed. My bed, but also *not* my bed. It's the same...but different.

The floor, which usually has that fake hardwood flooring is rough under my bare feet. The boards are warped.

"Hello?" I call out. My voice is muted, yet somehow echoey, in this empty place.

I go to the door, which is closed, which doesn't have a hook on the back where I hang my purses and my favorite hoodie.

It's just a standard white door. Around the edges of it in the cracks and creases it's gray with age. The doorknob is cold in my hand. I open the door.

This is my house but not my house.

I step into the hallway.

It looks longer than the hallway I'm used to seeing when I come out of my room. And yet it's the same hallway. Except the floorboards are warped, bending up at the ends. Tripping hazards. The walls are crusted with age, wallpaper peeling and falling off.

I call out again. My voice breaks the silence in this house. My house, but not my house.

The unbearable silence. I realized then that I'm really alone. I am utterly alone.

I had dreamed of being alone for so long. And now that it's here, it's frightening.

I don't know where my family went. And, oddly, I miss the cacophony of their voices. Each one trying to be heard over the last.

No one ever hears me though. No one ever heard me when they were here.

Where are they? Where am I? This place that's my house but not my house.

I go from room to room searching for my brothers and sisters. Their doors are all locked. I jiggle the handles and push my full weight against the doors. They won't open. I hammer my fists against the hollow wood.

No one answers. No familiar faces peek out. No one is home.

I venture out to the living room, expecting to see them all sitting quietly, draped on the furniture with their headphones plugged into their ears, tablets propped on their laps, and at the same time I know they won't be there.

The furniture in the living room slouches, old and worn. The bright orange L-shaped sectional that delighted my mom is gray. The green curtains, a different shade of gray. Everything is gray.

I look at my hands. Even I'm gray.

I go to the kitchen. The dining room table is covered in food leftover from a feast. My stomach growls. When I get closer, it's all rotten.

But there are no flies. No rancid smells.

It's last night's Sunday dinner. Mom and Dad always go out of their way to create a big dinner for us on Sundays. Even though the older kids work later shifts at their menial jobs, and the little kids don't appreciate what good food really tastes like.

They all want food from the places the older kids work at.

I loved Sunday dinners. Wait...did I?

I didn't. It was noise around a table. It was trying to be seen and heard over the cries and whines of the little kids because they didn't like what was on the table and wanted something else. The older kids talked about college applications with hubris in their voices. In the way they held their heads.

And me. trying to be heard over them all. Trying to tell my family—what was I trying to tell them?

I open the cupboards in the kitchen. They're bare. I open the refrigerator. No light comes on.

I flip the light switch on the wall. The lights don't work. The power is out. Yet there's some light filtering from somewhere. This cold gray light.

I try to venture outside, to see the sun in this cold place.

The back door is locked. I can't unlock it. I twist the doorknob lock and try again. The knob turns but the door won't open. I check the deadbolt.

I engage it. I disengage it. The door won't open no matter which way the deadbolt is turned. With shaking hands, I push the curtains on the back door window to the side.

Outside there's nothing. Just blackness. My hand finds the switch for the back porch light, and I know it won't work, but I flip it anyway.

It does work. But the light doesn't penetrate the darkness outside this house.

This house that is mine, but not mine.

I am alone. I am utterly alone.

I scream.

No one is there to hear me.

The One You Feed

Leah stood in front of the house she and her husband had lived in for the past ten years. They'd bought it just months after getting married.

"It's a split-level," she remembered saying. "We're going to live in a split-level tree, just like the Berenstain Bears!"

She remembered being so excited about this, like being a cartoon bear from her childhood would solve any problem that might arise in their marriage. Including the green-eyed monster called Jealousy.

Drew and Miggy were Stan's friends from college. They'd all known each other long before Leah and Stan met and married. Miggy was his best man—well, woman—at their wedding. She was the type of trendy, hip, popular girl Leah despised in high school *and* college, but once Leah got to know Miggy, Leah discovered Miggy was actually a big fat dork and she loved her even more because of it. Miggy called Stan and Leah "Stanleah" in one of those cutesy combined names.

When Stan introduced Leah to Miggy and Drew, they'd quickly accepted Leah, turning their triad into a quartet.

Drew and Miggy were the type of couple who bickered openly and with zero qualms, no matter the company in attendance. Leah often wondered why they were still together. She asked Miggy once, only because the wine had gone straight to her head and she asked before even thinking.

"Two words, Leah. Great sex," Miggy told her, half drunk on Rosé. "And the cunnilingus." She said the word in a silky whisper and waggled her tongue between her spread fingers lasciviously.

They were on her and Drew's lavish back patio. She'd leaned into Leah in that we've-been-girlfriends-all-our-lives kind of way that made Leah feel like maybe they could be. They were sitting side by side on a swinging loveseat amid huge potted plants and trees. Miggy's sanctuary. Leah had been so jealous of their house, their backyard oasis, all of it. It was just so lovely.

They hung out a lot, the four of them. They even went on vacation together. Beach vacations where Miggy flaunted her perfect body in the tiniest bikinis and Leah stayed in the shade, covered from head to toe.

"Come play volleyball with us," Miggy shouted from the net, bopping a volleyball up in the air and catching it over and over. She grinned in Leah's direction, sun drunk and tan. The tan only made her physique that much more attractive.

Leah didn't play volleyball. She wasn't sporty. She wasn't tan. She kept her body covered not only because of a healthy fear of sun damage and skin cancer, but also because she'd never lost the fat and happy weight she'd gained their first year of marriage, nine years ago.

She'd always had a negative relationship with her looks. Specifically her body. Every part of it.

"Come on, Leah," Stan called, but he wasn't looking at her. His face was pointed in Miggy's direction, and though he wore sunglasses, Leah could tell he was looking at Miggy's perfectly toned ass.

"Get some vitamin D," Drew shouted. Then laughed raucously, because they'd all joked about vitamin D being dick, and then how Drew's name also started with D, so essentially getting vitamin D had become the nickname for Drew's penis. "I don't mean it like that." He self-consciously adjusted his swim trunks, and Leah felt her face flush despite the supposed innocence of the adjustment.

Leah put her book down—she hated beach vacations because of the sand and the sun and just all of it, but she'd relished the idea of lying around reading all day—and stepped out of the shade.

"Yeah!" Miggy shouted, pumping her fist into the air. "Take off that cover-up. Get some sun on that hot bod." She grinned at Leah, half her face obscured by trendy aviator sunglasses that made Leah look like a giant insect when she tried them on. "And that hat. It'll fall off when you dive for the ball I'm going to spike over the net." Miggy laughed in a fake obnoxious way Leah had never liked. It was a laugh she used whenever she was in a show-off kind of mood, after having a couple drinks.

Miggy always said things like that about Leah's body, or her hair, or her face, or anything about her. It should have made Leah feel cool and confident, but it made her feel like it was a big fat joke at her expense.

Get some sun on that hot bod. As if.

The sand was hot on the soles of Leah's feet. She didn't like this peer pressure to expose her body to the sun's harmful rays. She peered up at the sky and tugged her cover-up around her tighter.

"I just have to go to the bathroom really quick," she called. "Then I'll come play." She picked her way to the walkway at the edge of the sand that would take her to the hotel lobby—an open-air reprieve from the harsh sun and the heat.

She glanced over her shoulder just in time to see Miggy throw an arm around Stan and try to wrestle him to the ground. Drew threw his head back with open-mouthed laughter, hands on his thrust-forward hips as if he wanted his D to join in their fun.

As long as Drew and Miggy are together, I have nothing to worry about. She told herself this at least once every time they hung out.

Leah bypassed the lobby and the beach bathrooms and went up to her and Stan's room. She pulled off her cover-up and her ridiculous wide-brimmed hat and looked at her body in the full-length mirror.

Pale, pasty, doughy. She could pass as a lump of pizza dough with legs. Every part of her looked flabby and saggy compared to Miggy's tightly packed, toned, and tanned body.

She knew she shouldn't compare—every body is beautiful, after all—but how could she go out on the beach and pretend to be happy bouncing around in the sun when she hated the way she looked? How she hated herself for looking this way and not being able to change it?

"Put your sorries in a sack," she muttered. "Just go out there. No one will care." There were plenty of other women out there on the beach tanning in skimpy bathing suits who would sell their souls to the devil to have Leah's body.

She lifted her chin and slathered on some SPF 50 sunblock, pulled her hair into a ponytail, crammed a visor on her head to at least block *most* of her face, and lifted her chin. She met her eyes in the mirror.

Her lip trembled.

"No," she whispered. A tear fell. "Stop it." She completely broke down, sobbing into her hands. She grabbed the couple inches of flab on her belly and squeezed it hard. Then she cried because it hurt. She punched herself in the hips. "Stop crying, you idiot," she said to her reflection through gritted teeth.

Someone knocked on the door.

"Leah?"

Stan.

Shit.

She wiped her eyes and pulled her cover-up back on, donned her sunglasses to hide her wet lashes. She opened the door.

"Hey," she said. "I was just—"

"You okay?"

She nodded, bit her lip, shook her head *no*. Stan stepped toward her and embraced her.

His hugs were the best hugs. His arms so strong around her. The warmth of his body, the scent of his sun-heated skin. In the mirror, she was a porcelain doll in his tan Ken Doll arms.

"Let's do it," she said, pulling him toward the bed.

"Miggy's waiting. And Drew." He cleared his throat.

"Come on, Stan. It's vacation. They can wait. They probably already wandered off down the beach to that bar again anyway."

He grinned at her. Lifted her easily by her ass. She wrapped her legs around him and they fell onto the bed.

At dinner, Drew ordered up a round of the island's specialty cocktail.

"I love your dress," Miggy said. "So flattering." Her eyes, heavily lashed with fake eyelashes, looked Leah up and down. Leah looked down at her dress, as if she'd forgotten what she put on.

She wanted to say, "oh, this old thing?" like in the movies and pretend like she got compliments all the time, but instead she tucked a strand of hair behind her ear and said, "Thanks. Yours is pretty, too."

Miggy wore a sequined dress that barely covered her ass.

"It's so *old*," she said. A variant of, "This old thing?"

"It's beautiful."

Leah was surprised to see Miggy's cheeks flush. But it could have just been the lighting.

Later that evening, after several of the specialty cocktails, they sat in low chairs around a fire pit, laughing about old times. Leah listened to her husband, sitting *across* the fire from her for some reason, recount tales of his and Miggy's college shenanigans.

Her mind drifted off to wondering—as it always did when they talked about the old times—if Stan and Miggy were ever a thing. And if not an actual thing, had they ever hooked up, just once, just to see. She found it incredibly hard to believe they'd only been friends throughout college.

"What are our thoughts on polyamory again?" Miggy laughed in the sexy throaty way she did after too many beverages.

Leah looked up. Miggy was looking directly at her. She winked. Miggy sat on Stan's lap, Stan's hand on her hip so close to her ass.

Her barely covered ass.

Leah leaped to her feet, grabbed Miggy by her perfectly lived-in highlighted hair, and threw her into the fire. Miggy screamed and flailed, unable to stand with her ridiculous clompy wedge sandals—who wears wedge sandals to the beach?

Leah watched her burn while Stan and Drew cried out, screaming into the fire, unable to help—

Drew chuckled, pulling Leah out of her sick thoughts. She shook herself and looked up. Miggy still stared at her, though her smile had drooped.

"Come on, Miggs. Leave Stan alone." Drew held out his hand to her. "We aren't keen on polyamory. That's our take, remember?" Drew winked at her, and she grinned at him.

"Get off him," Leah said in a voice so low and so guttural she wasn't even sure it came out of her throat.

"It's just a joke," Stan said.

Miggy stood and smoothed down the fabric of her dress. Stan turned away. Was he hiding something? A raging boner, perhaps? Leah glared at him. Miggy tottered in her strappy wedge heels, arms askew. Drew lurched to his feet and caught her by the wrist. He pulled her against him.

"Come sit on *my* lap. We'll talk about how you need more vitamin D in your diet." He laughed raucously, but Miggy pulled away.

"I'm gonna go walk on the beach. Anyone want to join me?" She looked at Leah, eyes wide and hopeful.

Leah stood. Miggy's eyes brightened. Leah turned and stormed away.

"Leah," Stan called. But did he follow her? No. He didn't. And part of Leah wondered if he was just going to go walk on the beach with Miggy. Maybe trip and pull her into the surf where they'd tumble about trying to get up, both drunk on specialty cocktails and unable to get their footing with the soft wet sand. Her hair dangling in his face—

"Stop," she whispered to herself. "He won't do that."

As long as Miggy and Drew are together...

Leah thought of that vacation while staring up at their marital house. The house they'd built their life in.

The trouble started a month ago. Stan came home from work, cell phone pressed to his ear. He made sounds as if trying to interrupt the speaker on the other end. He kissed the top of Leah's head and pointed at the phone.

"Miggy," he mouthed.

Leah could hear the tinny sound of Miggy's voice wailing through the phone.

Her mouth went dry. Miggy didn't cry. Not that Leah had ever seen anyway. This could not be good.

She imagined Drew in the hospital or dead. Her throat dried. Her heart started to pound. If Drew didn't make it...

Stan finally got off the phone.

"What is it?" Leah asked, unable to keep the urgency from her voice. "What's happened to Miggy?"

Stan looked up at her. "She left Drew."

Miggy started hanging around more. Showing up, popping in, always with wine and wanting to have a drink or two or three—she always said that with a giggle and a wink in Leah's direction.

Leah wasn't much of a drinker, but she did it so Miggy and Stan wouldn't be alone together at any point. She stayed up late, even though she had work early in the morning, so they would not be alone together. She did everything possible she could think of, so they wouldn't be alone together, even inviting Miggy to help her in the kitchen, even though Miggy didn't know her way around a knife, let alone the complicated charcuterie and cheese boards Leah threw together.

To her credit, Miggy seemed to make it a point to sit far away from Stan and closer to Leah, as if showing Leah, *look there's nothing to worry about. You can trust me with your husband.*

"Stan, why don't you just go to bed so me and Leah can

have some girl time," Miggy said once, leaning into Leah in that friendly way she did. Leah was the one who wanted to go to bed. Stan gave Miggy a strange look and shook his head. He met Leah's eyes.

That night they had the worst fight of their marriage.

"Does she have to come over *every* night?" Leah asked, putting the used wine glasses in the sink.

"She's lonely and needs us, Leah." Stan handed her a small pile of appetizer dishes they'd used for snacks. Leah set them in the bottom of the sink and swiped a strand of hair behind her ear.

"Can't she be lonely and needy with someone else?" She met Stan's eyes.

Stan rolled his. "She doesn't *have* anyone else."

Leah found that hard to believe.

"What's the big deal, anyway?"

It started out innocuous enough, but soon she was shouting about how she didn't trust Miggy's motives, a hot single woman on the prowl. Stan didn't respond, which sent Leah into a flurry of slamming cupboards—they were soft-close so the effect was lost, but she tried hard to make them slam.

She emptied the silverware tray from the clean dishwasher, throwing the utensils into the drawer where they clattered against each other.

Stan, always calm and unshakable, didn't respond.

"Don't you have *anything* to say?" she shouted.

Stan shrugged and shook his head. "You're being ridiculous."

But Miggy didn't show her face around their house for a few days after that.

Then Leah came home and Miggy's car was in the driveway. Leah's core temperature dropped about ten degrees. She shuddered and pulled in next to Miggy.

She didn't lock her car with the fob—it would make a beeping sound—oh no. She wanted to catch them in the act. Her cold core instantly heated as she thought of walking in on them in the throes of their adulterous violations.

Leah opened the front door just enough to slip inside. She crept up the stairs, ears tuned to any sounds. Cries of ecstasy, moans of passion.

Murmurs came from the kitchen. She frowned. The kitchen?

She crept in that direction.

"We have to tell her," Stan said. "She needs to know."

"No. No, not yet. I can't. It's been a secret for too long now. What will she think?"

Stan's frustrated sound. Leah could see him throw his arms up, face pointed at the ceiling. That's how he always did frustration. Overly dramatic asshole.

"When? When can we tell her?"

"Tell me what?" Leah stepped into the kitchen.

Stan and Miggy froze as if they'd been caught doing much worse than talking about secrets.

"Tell me what, Stan?" Leah asked again, her teeth clenched so hard her jaw hurt. She flicked her eyes to Miggy. Miggy shied away. "Miggy? What do you *not* want to tell me?"

Miggy held up her hands, her mouth forming the shape of a placating word.

"Get out." Leah pointed to the door. Also overly dramatic, she knew. "Get out of my house."

"Leah, be reasonable—"

She turned on Stan. "Reasonable?" Her voice came out high-pitched, riding the edge of a scream that was bound to come out if Miggy didn't get the *fuck* out of her house. She wheeled around.

"*Get out of my house.*" This time she did scream it.

Miggy, tears in her eyes, scurried out of the kitchen, shoulders up around her ears like a beaten dog.

"Miggy," Stan called. He glared at Leah. "Uncalled for."

"Go ahead, Stan," Leah said. "Go after her." Leah waved her hand toward the door. She didn't know when the tears had come, but they spilled down her cheeks. "If you do, don't come back."

Stan gave Leah a strange look—some mixture of disappointment and a general misunderstanding. He rounded the island. Leah prepared to be enveloped in his embrace, coddled, told there was nothing to worry about, Miggy just didn't want to tell Leah about some horrible secret past. It had nothing to do with the two of them together, or their adultery.

He brushed past her.

"Uncalled for," he muttered as he traipsed down the stairs.

"Don't fucking come back," Leah shrieked.

The door slammed. She collapsed into a sobbing heap. A car door slammed. An engine started.

Leah got up and hurried to the front door, out onto the porch, down into the driveway.

The cool evening air chilled her hot cheeks. Leah turned and looked at her house. Her Berenstain Bear house.

She went inside and closed the door behind her, leaned against it with her eyes shut. Tears dribbled down her cheeks. She slid to the floor and dropped her face into her hands, her sobs the only sound in the house.

She woke curled on the welcome mat, her head resting on Stan's stinky running shoes. Darkness had enveloped the house, save for the light from the living room at the top of the stairs that came on automatically at 9 p.m.

A whine, a whimper, not her own, came from somewhere nearby.

Leah sat up. The stairs leading down to the lower level dropped into darkness, and inside that darkness glowed two green eyes.

Leah clambered to her feet, pressing against the door. She fumbled for her phone, but it wasn't on her. It was still in her car. She'd left everything in her car so she could sneak in and catch Stan and Miggy—

The eyes blinked. Another whimper. It sounded like a dog.

"We don't have a dog," she whispered. The eyes crept forward and came partway up the stairs. It *was* a dog. "How'd you get in here?" She crouched and held out her hand. "Come on, I won't hurt you." *Please don't hurt me.*

Didn't rabid animals get confused? Wasn't that part of the disease? The reason they turned on the people they loved?

Or wandered into the wrong home, perhaps?

She didn't think the dog had rabies.

The dog came up the last few steps. It towered over her, but not in an unnatural way.

If Leah were ever to get a purebred dog, she always wanted an Irish wolfhound. This one was albino. Its wiry fur pure white. Its eyes red. It hung its head and whimpered.

It looked how Leah felt. Leah peered past the dog into the dark basement.

She thought she heard something moving around down there in the darkness of Stan's wine cellar.

The basement of a split-level wasn't supposed to be a scary place since half of it was above ground. There were windows, for Chrissakes. But here she was, a grown woman, peering into that black darkness wondering if it was always that dark. Wondering what was moving around down there. Feeling an overwhelming sense of *get the hell out*.

Maybe the dog's owner was down there, too. Pillaging the precious wine collection.

"Who's there?" Leah called, rising from her crouched position, pulling the dog's head against her.

No one answered. She wished Stan was there. He would go down and check things out.

Leah stood taller, straightened her shoulders. She didn't need a man to protect her. She could do it herself. She took a step toward the stairs leading down into the basement level.

The dog slid in front of her, hackles raised, and bared its teeth. They were all sharp and pointed. Nightmarish. Too many of them. Saliva dripped from its mouth. Black tears streamed down the sides of its muzzle. It trembled. With aggression or fear, Leah didn't know.

It turned with graceful movements reserved for large animals and loped down the stairs into the darkness below.

Leah put her hand to her forehead and found it beaded with sweat. She felt cold and shivery.

She never enjoyed being home alone. Not even when she had plans to get things done and dreamed of some alone time. Not even during the day. Every sound of the house settling sounded abnormal and set her on high alert. Did it always sound that way? Was that a *different* sound?

She retrieved a baseball bat from the hall closet where Stan kept his stinky sporting gear, and went back down to the landing. She flicked on the light.

"I'm coming down," she called. "I don't want to hurt you. But I will if I have to."

She crept down the stairs, baseball bat cocked on her shoulder.

Rows upon rows of wine bottles glittered in the light. She walked up and down the rows, breathing slowly in through her nose out through her mouth. She passed Stan's beloved older wines, ones that had been aging for a while now, green glass covered in a thick layer of dust and maybe mold.

The dog was nowhere to be seen, and neither was there anyone else. Leah went to the door connecting the wine cellar to the garage. It wasn't latched. She jerked the door open. A breeze came through from the opposite side of the garage where the window was also open. Wide open.

Leah closed the garage door and locked it as a shivering tremble traveled over her. The dog got in through the garage, which means there probably had been someone down there.

She ran up the stairs. The farthest point from the top of the stairs was the kitchen. But when she got there, the sight of it ripped the freshly congealed scab off the proverbial wound.

We have to tell her...she needs to know.

Leah swung the bat with a scream and smashed a bowl of fruit. Oranges, apples, and a banana flew onto the floor and rolled every which way. She shoved dirty dishes on the counter into the sink, where some of them broke or broke other things—beloved wine glasses—that were innocent bystanders.

She picked up Stan's computer and chucked it across the room, where it crashed against the wall and fell to the floor in more than a few pieces. There was a dent in the wall where it struck.

Her heart pounded. Her face felt hot. Her brain was on fire.

Down below, the dog yelped, whimpered, cried out.

There was no dog down there. Leah gritted her teeth, but stopped and listened, breath heaving in and out. A cluster of hair sucked in and out of her nostril. She grabbed it and yanked it out with an angry grunt.

Silence. Except for the clock ticking on the wall. She ripped it down and smashed it.

A yelp from the basement.

"Dog?" Leah ran to the top of the stairs. She couldn't see down into the basement around the bend at the bottom, though. "Dog?" Her voice was a squeak.

A voiceless sound rose from the dark.

Dread's panicky grip took her heart in its clutches. Leah stood frozen in place, gasping for breath, her hands gripping the banisters so hard it hurt her palms.

She'd checked every row, every corner. Where could they have been hiding?

The sound came again.

It wasn't the dog. It was something else.

Something terrifying. Something she couldn't see but she could *feel*, and it was made of dread and everything terrifying she'd ever experienced. She suddenly had to pee, but still she couldn't move.

Whatever it was, she didn't want to see it. She didn't want to hear it again. The sound of it—

She took a few deep breaths. Her hands released the banisters. She backed away from the top of the stairs.

"Dog?" she whimpered. The way it had cried—she'd never heard an animal make sounds like that. "If you hurt that dog again—" She shook her head. "Get out of my house, whoever you are! Get out or I'll call the police!"

The clack of claws on the tile on the landing. Leah crawled to the top of the stairs and ventured a peek.

The dog stood on the landing, great head sagging. The red eyes peered up at her. Its sides heaved with each panted breath. Saliva, black and viscous, dripped from its open mouth. It held its ears pinned back against the sides of its head.

It looked beaten, punished. It looked despondent. The black tears had stained the snow-white fur around its muzzle.

"Come here," Leah whispered. She held out her hand. "I'll keep you safe."

The dog didn't come. It looked up at her, then down the stairs. It gave her one last forlorn look, took a deep breath, let out a breathy whimper, and trotted back to the darkness.

Leah found the bat on the kitchen floor and picked it up. She imagined finding whoever was down there hiding in her basement and beating the living shit out of them.

Maybe it's Stan, too afraid to come up.

She didn't care that Stan didn't have a dog. In her mind it was him. She could claim self-defense. All alone at home. Strange sounds. The window open, the door open.

"I thought he was an intruder, Officer," she whispered, choking up on the bat.

Leah didn't bother turning on the light this time.

"I couldn't see, the light was out, I thought I was being attacked," she whispered her defense to the empty house.

At the bottom of the stairs, she listened while her eyes adjusted to the dark.

A white form stood just at the entrance to the wine cellar. The dog, of course. It let out a low growling whine. Bottles clinked against each other. Leah flicked her eyes beyond the dog.

A shape, crouched and wild, sat at the end of the main aisle in the darkness beyond the dog. Leah took a step back, almost dropped the bat.

She didn't want to look at it. Seeing it there like that filled her with indescribable terror. But she couldn't pull her eyes away.

A car came down the street, headlights flashing across and through the shelves of wine bottles. The light traveled over the crouched shape as the car rounded the bend outside their house. The car stopped. The headlights poised on the thing's face.

Leah shrieked. Her bladder threatened to release.

The thing wore her face stretched into a rictus of evil anger, brows furrowed so deep they became one with the bridge of the nose, lips pulled up at the corners so high, they nearly collided with the eyes.

The dog let out another growling whine. It barked and lunged at Leah.

Leah ran up the stairs, the baseball bat forgotten on the stone floor. As she rounded the corner on the landing, the doorbell rang.

She shrieked again and fell against the banister.

Leah's heart beat behind her eyes, darkness dimming the edges of her vision with each pulse. A strange calm came over her, though her head rang and it felt like her brain would burst out of her skull through her ears.

The bell rang again. Leah reached a hand toward the knob, gripped it. She peered through the peep hole.

Miggy stood on the doorstep, eyes red-rimmed. Mascara ran down her cheeks. The false eyelashes on her left eye askew.

If she knew she would cry, why even put those ridiculous things on?

The hatred toward this sobbing woman—how dare she come back and crying? *Crying?*—bubbled in Leah's gut. It traveled up her body. Her cheeks ignited. Her temples throbbed.

Leah ripped the door open. "What do you want?" her voice growled.

Miggy's face contorted with renewed tears. "Please,

Leah. I'm sorry. Can I please come in? Can I please—" She lifted a thick letter-sized envelope.

Behind Leah, something down below thrashed in the darkness. Bottles rattled.

That thing. That crouching thing moving around.

The dog barked, but the bark was cut short by a pained yipe.

Leah glanced over her shoulder. The thing that wore her face squatted there, only just visible. It gave Leah a slow dip of its chin.

Leah clenched her teeth, turned back to Miggy, and opened the door wider.

Miggy brushed inside, her signature scent trailing after her. Leah would forever tie Vanilla Musk to this wretched feeling of betrayal. Her once friend stepped up the stairs as if they might break under her insubstantial weight.

Leah gave the thing one last narrow-eyed look and followed Miggy upstairs to the kitchen.

"Leah," Miggy said, sniffling. Snorting snot back up into her sinuses.

"Miggy," Leah said, her voice calm but acidic.

"I just, I—" She looked down at the envelope in her hands. "I wrote you something." She placed the envelope on the counter between them.

"I feel like you need some wine," Leah said, voice still tinged with acid. "Would you mind going down to the basement to get us a bottle? Anything you want. Even from Stan's *best* shelf."

Miggy would know which one was Stan's best shelf, wouldn't she? Leah was sure during one of their trysts he probably fucked her down there, back against the butts of the moldy, dusty bottles. Miggy probably had round dust circles on her back, or ass, or tits, or all of the above afterward. They probably laughed and laughed about it. Stan probably wiped her down with a washcloth. Or did they cleanse each other under the dual shower heads in the master *en suite*?

"Sh-Sure," Miggy said. She wiped at her eyes as she moved past Leah, brushing against her. Not a shoulder check, but the way a cat winds around its owner's ankles. Leah touched her shoulder where Miggy's scented skin touched her.

Leah listened to the traitorous bitch descend, eyes on the white envelope on the counter. It had Leah's name on it. She picked it up.

"Who is that?" Miggy's voice from the basement, so clear Leah thought Miggy had come back upstairs already. "Leah? Is that you—but you were just upstairs—Leah!"

Leah turned when a shrill scream hit her ears. The dog yipped and howled like a coyote after a rabbit, only the sound wasn't one of excitement of the hunt.

Leah pulled a letter out, unfolded the pages.

Dear Leah, it read.

Leah's eyes traveled over Miggy's looping handwriting —of course she had a teenager's flirtatious cursive—and as she read, her hand started to shake. Her heart started to soften. Her eyes filled with tears.

It was never Stan I wanted. It was always you. I have loved you since the day we met. Drew is and always has been a cover for who I really am. A cover because my parents would never understand. They'd cut me off, they'd disown me. Drew doesn't even know my secret attraction to women. No one knows except Stan, and Stan only knows because of college and a time when he saw—

Leah skipped ahead, unable to stop her eyes.

You are the most beautiful woman I have ever met, inside and out. So confident. I wish I could be more like you.

I know you aren't like me, that you love Stan and men in general, but I had to tell you. There is nothing between me and Stan. I've only ever wanted to have something with you.

The screams from the basement had dwindled to quiet whimpering moans.

I'm sorry I didn't tell you sooner. I just wasn't sure how you would take it. I didn't want to risk losing you, even as a friend.

Leah put the letter down, tears in her eyes. It had to be a ploy, right? A way to get Leah on her side so she could still come around and see Stan? Get *his* comfort?

She thought back to the past weeks when she'd come over. How Miggy sat next to Leah. The vacation when Miggy wanted Leah to walk with her on the beach. How she complimented Leah's dress and *hot bod*.

All the times she'd chosen to sit next to Leah, to lean against her in that old-girlfriends kind of way. How Leah wanted to be Miggy's best friend.

She'd wanted to be Leah's maid of honor, even, but Leah already had a friend in mind for the job, which is why she ended up being Stan's best woman.

"Miggy?" Leah cried the name and ran down the stairs. "Miggy!"

At the bottom of the stairs, Miggy lay still in the dusky darkness of the wine cellar. A puddle of dark fluid surrounded her. The baseball bat lay next to her body.

The crouched and wild creature was nowhere to be seen.

"Miggy." Leah ran to Miggy's side, cupped her smooth cheek. Miggy's eyes opened and swiveled around wildly. They landed on Leah's face, but didn't seem to focus. Her throat worked. A trickle of blood spilled from the corner of her mouth.

The dog came out of the shadows, limping, drooping. Its mouth hung open, tongue lolling.

"I tried to warn you," a voice from vocal chords not meant for language came from the dog's open mouth.

The front door banged open.

"Leah? Miggy?" Stan's voice on the landing. Footsteps on the stairs, traveling across the floor above them.

The dog stepped closer until its nose nearly touched Leah's. She looked into its sad eyes and her heart shattered. The dog circled behind her and lay by her side, resting its head in her lap, enveloping her in a shroud of deep sadness.

Leah wept quietly over Miggy.

"I'm sorry, Miggy," Leah whispered. "I could have loved you...I could have. I should have. Even as a friend. I should have trusted you—"

"Leah?" Stan's voice. "Oh my God, Leah. Is that blood —" He backed away, hitting the shelf behind him. A bottle of wine slid to the floor and smashed. Deep garnet fluid mixed with Miggy's blood. "Miggy?" His voice a squeak now.

"I didn't do this," Leah sobbed. "I didn't do this." How could she tell him it was a weird creature version of her who did this to their friend. How could she tell him?

The dog followed Leah to the police car, watched as the officer held a hand to the top of her head and ducked her inside. The ambulance took Miggy away. Stan stood at the bottom of the porch steps leading up to the front door of their Berenstain Bear house.

As the police cruiser pulled away with Leah inside, the dog loped after it until the car got up to speed and outpaced the poor ragged creature.

Leah, empty inside. No sadness. No anger. No love. Nothing. Just empty.

She saw them everywhere after that. Big drooping dogs crying black tears from their red eyes. They followed the women in the prison around, moping, shuffling along behind them, heads lowered, tails unwagging.

And some of the women had big wicked grins frozen on their faces. Eyebrows low. Leah stayed away from them. They were the ones who got in fights most often.

Stan came to visit her. Miggy survived. It was touch and go for a while. Brain swelling, comatose, there was talk of her never recovering. Then she did recover.

"She said she was talking to you in the kitchen, and you sent her to get some wine, and you were also in the basement?" He shook his head. "Anyway, she's not pressing charges." Stan didn't smile at this. Neither did Leah. "Fuck. She loves you so much she won't even press charges. You almost fucking *killed* her."

He slammed the phone receiver on the hook, pushed away from the little table beyond the plexiglass, and stormed out. A black wolfhound followed him out, leaving a puddle of sad black ichor behind it.

Another month passed.

Miggy came to visit, head shaved where they had to stitch her scalp back together. She made it look fashionable. They got to meet in the visiting room. Just the two of them.

"I don't know what to say to you," Leah said. "I'm sorry just doesn't cut it. I wish I could hug you. I'm so glad you're okay."

Miggy smiled at her and didn't say anything. She sat there smiling. Ten seconds, twenty. Then, her face—oh God, her face—contorted into an evil rictus of a grin. Her brows folded low over her eyes.

Behind her, a gray Irish wolfhound with red eyes and black tears dripping down its muzzle whined.

The Strangel

The Stranger rode in on a horse—odd in these modern times—wearing a blood-soaked dress. The fabric of the bodice gaped open in places, exposing her porcelain white skin gashed with injuries caused by blades. Her horse, head low, took slow unsteady steps, legs quaking with fatigue. The Stranger, slumped in her saddle, canted sideways and slid off onto the ground. Her body smacked the pavement with a sickening slap of flesh on asphalt. The horse collapsed one step later, let out a long loud sigh, and died.

At first, no one approached. The onlookers—so-called innocent bystanders—looked around at each other in a stunned and awkward silence.

"Is she dead?" someone asked.

"Is there a doctor here?" someone else asked.

A woman in scrubs raised her hand but made no move toward the Stranger.

The Stranger gasped. The doctor took a tentative step, then quickly ran to the Stranger's side.

"I have a message to share," the Stranger said. "A message that will save you."

"Me?" The doctor looked up to see if anyone had heard. They had all stepped closer, curious, but not close enough to be held accountable should something go sideways.

The Stranger shook her head. "A message for the world." She coughed. A thin line of blood trickled from her mouth. "It will save you all."

"Save us?" The doctor looked around again at her neighbors. Faces she'd seen shuffling to the mailboxes with names she did not know. Faces matched to house colors or certain cars that drove down their street at the same time every weekday. The Stranger spoke again. The doctor returned her attention to the Stranger's face.

"I have traveled the country for four years searching for someone to hear me. But the fear in their hearts would not allow them to trust me. They cut me with their words."

The doctor looked over the Stranger's bloodied bodice, at the gaping wounds inside the torn fabric.

"These were caused by words?" The doctor could not keep the skepticism—the disbelief—from her voice.

The Stranger nodded. "No one would listen," she whispered. A tear leaked from her eye. Her eyes unfocused, then focused again. "My message is borne of love, not fear." Her eyes closed. "It will save you all, but no one will hear it."

"I'm listening," the doctor said, trained to be compassionate toward the dying whether she felt it or not.

The Stranger took one last shuddering breath. The doctor looked up at the neighbor-strangers around her. They'd gathered closer still. Tragedy drew a crowd after all.

"Look." One of them pointed.

The doctor looked down, leaped backward. A white light rose from the Strangers chest. Once it had gained altitude, it expanded into the shape of the woman lying on the ground. Great wings spread from her back. She looked around at all of them, shielding their eyes from the brilliance of her glow.

Then she looked up, flapped her great wings, and disappeared into the clouds.

"What did she say?" someone asked.

"What caused her wounds?" someone else asked.

"She said no one would listen to her. That she could save us all, but no one would listen." The doctor still peered up at the sky.

"Save us from what?" someone with a snarky voice asked.

"We don't need saving," someone else said with disgust.

The doctor looked down at the dead Stranger, at the wounds caused by words, the blood-soaked fabric, her horse already attracting flies, and shrugged. A tear coursed down her own cheek.

Ourselves, she thought but did not say for fear of what the others would think, say, or do to her.

Hurry Scurry

SOMETHING IS INSIDE THE WALLS

All night long I tried to sleep
But in the wall was a creep a peep
A scratch a scurry
something in a hurry
A thump a bump
A misshapen lump
Standing in my doorway
I tried to scream
No sound emerged
No flashlight beam
Adrenaline surged
Who is that standing in my
        doorway?
Nefarious something. No time
        to pray
The figure shifts, becomes obscured
by deeper darkness and shadows
        blurred
A scratch a scurry

something in a hurry
a thump a bump
a misshapen lump
Standing at the foot of my bed
I throw the covers over my head
Wishing hoping it will not notice
Wishing for this thing of dread
To leave before I feel death's kiss
A gentle jostle upon the bed
The covers shift, I'm filled with
    dread
Tears squeeze from my closed eyes
Waiting for my demise
A scratch a scurry
Something in a hurry
A thump a bump
A misshapen lump
Lying next to me on my bed.
A voice from Hell's bowels speaks
No scratch no scurry
Not a creep not a peep
There is no hurry
A growling sound made of terror
I might have died had I been fairer
My trembling form under blankets
    huddles
The creature says, you look scared.
    Would you like some cuddles?

Perfectly Safe

ABANDONED BUILDING

As soon as Connie entered the building, she knew she'd made a huge mistake. But she needed the money. She would have been an idiot to pass on this job.

She read objects for people on the corner of Broadway and Lindon, doing well enough to pay the rent and put food in her belly.

And by "read," she could close her eyes, hold an object handed to her by a customer, and discern through some otherworldly images who had owned the piece and—sometimes—what happened to them. The best was when she could see them so clearly she could give details about what the person wore—usually whatever they'd worn in while lying in their coffins—and sometimes, if she was really lucky, they would say something.

The voices never truly reached her ears, but she had gotten really good at lip reading, having had a head injury that left her with severe tinnitus. A constant rushing sound in her ears often muffled the voice of someone speaking right in front of her. Sometimes she wondered if it wasn't static from the Beyond. Like a radio station having trouble tuning in.

Sometimes, at night, she heard things in that constant roar.

She hadn't wanted to get into street performing, but her mother, who was far more adept at reading, had talked her into it, knowing Connie had the gift. They were a great team. Connie's mom's ability seemed to amplify her own.

Once she really got into it, Connie dreamed of opening a shop of her own where she and her mom could work together. The kind of place that sold crystals and tarot cards and candles of all different colors for different purposes. The readings would be the side gig within the store. A way to get people to come inside. Or maybe the trinkets would be the side thing.

Burn this candle to ward off that...wear this crystal to bring peace...

Posters declaring people could talk to their loved ones.

Connie had saved a bunch of her earnings from the street. Almost enough for a down payment on a little shop down the alley. It wasn't a great location, but they could keep the corner table up for a while and point people to the store.

But then her mother disappeared. And then came back. In a body bag.

Exposure, they said. Connie didn't buy it.

When she saw the body—to identify it—there were ligature marks on her neck, frozen for eternity in bruises on her mother's pale, bloodless flesh. She pointed it out, but no one listened. The cops often turned blind eyes to those less fortunate. Especially street performers who, in the eyes of the law, were all criminals. The cops also didn't care that her mother's favorite necklace was missing. A necklace her mother never took off. It was a protective amulet to ward away negative energy. She'd told Connie it was important to wear such protection in the occupation they were in. Connie wore one of her own, but she would have loved to inherit her mother's along with the history of protection it held within it.

Connie hadn't known her mother's financial instability until the bank came around to collect on the upside-down mortgage and the merchants, with whom her mother had overdue credit payments to make, knocked on the door demanding she pay her mother's balances.

Connie sold everything inside the little house—it wasn't much—and used her hard-earned savings to pay them all.

Why didn't she ask me for help? Connie wondered, doling out a large sum to a dress-maker.

All she had left after paying her mom's bills was enough for the cheapest casket they had at the funeral home. No services. No flowers. Just a wooden box to put in the ground.

The non-service was quick and painless for the most part. Connie cried those silent tears one cries when the heart can't be broken any further. The kind that just dribble down the cheeks without emphasis.

She stared at the hole, slowly filling with dirt, wishing she could have afforded the mahogany or cherry wood box for her mom. Something slick and shiny. But no. A pine box was what she got.

I could have taken it home, stained it, varnished it...

Connie's sister, Lindsay, showed up to watch them shovel dirt on top of the hole. Lindsay, who had had nothing to do with their mom for the past fifteen years, and who only looked down at Connie with disdain from her pedestal or high horse or maybe her high horse on a pedestal.

Lindsay shouted at Connie, blaming her for neglecting their mother, as if Connie had known anything about their mom's financial situation. Maybe she *should* have known. How did she not? Her mother hid it well, by buying things on credit.

"No regard for anyone but yourself. You've always been so selfish." Lindsay's voice cut through the muting fog— and the constant static—in Connie's head. She turned her tear-blurry eyes to her sister, made brief eye contact, turned on her heel, and walked out of the cemetery.

"Where are you going?"

A few weeks after her mother was laid to rest in the cold ground with no headstone but a wooden cross Connie had nailed together and painted white, she went back to reading objects, fearful she wouldn't do well now that her mom was gone.

Tourists congregated in the square at Broadway and Lindon. It was prime real estate to snag a corner there, and Connie's mom had been lucky enough to have found the corner after a previous performer had passed on. Connie wasn't sure if they'd passed on, or if they'd just retired from the hustle and grind of street performing. She assumed the former.

Regardless, Connie set up her table with their hand-painted sign and waited.

"You can read objects?" a man asked her. "What the hell does that mean? Objects don't got words on 'em."

Connie looked up from the section of newspaper she was reading. She met his eyes. He looked as dumb as he sounded. A mouth-breathing, ape-shouldered, eyes-too-close-together man in his twenties.

"If you give me an object," Connie said with her pleasant explanation voice, "I can tell you who owned it and sometimes more."

The man shoved his giant hands into his pockets and rummaged. He pulled out a button.

"Where'd this come from then?"

Connie opened her palm. The man dropped it in without touching her. She closed her eyes.

"This came from your pants. It's the second button from your fly. You broke it trying to get your drawers down to piss. You didn't make it."

She'd seen the same button on the front of his pants. She'd seen the hint of a dried stain, too. From there, she made up the story. This time to embarrass the object owner. She didn't have patience for idiots.

Sometimes her foolery guesses were spot-on. She opened her eyes to his red face.

"How'd you know?" he whispered.

She tapped her temple and raised an eyebrow, then pointed to the sign indicating he owed her twenty bucks.

He dug in his pocket and gave her a twenty with the faint scent of urine still lingering on it.

"If I bring you other things..." He paused and gulped. "Can you *tell* me other things?"

Connie nodded. "Twenty bucks per reading." She sat back down and opened her paper.

He came back once a day for a week before she told him not to come back. The last item he gave her was from a woman he'd hit. It was her clip-on earring, which had flown off her ear after he backhanded her. She didn't even take his money.

He walked away with a smirk.

"I should report you," she called after him.

"With what proof?" He held his hands out in a what-you-gonna-do-about-it kind of way.

Connie scowled at his back and watched him go. When she turned her attention back to the crowd, she jumped, startled by the person standing before her.

It was one of the other performers. A woman named Marlene, who did close-up magic tricks. Magical Marlene, her banner said.

"Oh, jeez, you scared me, Marl." Connie held out her hand and they did their not-so-secret handshake, which only consisted of two hand slaps and a fist bump. Only after their usual greeting did Connie realize Marlene looked pale. Frightened.

"What is it?" Connie asked. "Bruce?" Marlene had a love affair going on with one of the other performers, a juggler named Bruce, but he was rough-and-tumble and treated his women the same way. Connie scanned Marlene's exposed skin for bruises.

The Magician shook her head. "No, it's not Bruce." Her eyes filled with tears. "Not entirely, anyway."

"Then what?"

Marlene moved around Connie's table, pulled on her upper arm. Connie grabbed her cash box at the last second and allowed Marlene to drag her into the alley.

"I'm in trouble, Con," Marlene said. "I made some bad moves."

"With whom?" Connie asked.

"Bad folks," Marlene said. "Powerful. I cheated them, swindled them. Bruce and me both. It was a joint job, one of those types of cons where you earn someone's trust, then stab 'em in the back, only this time..." Her voice pinched and came out a squeak. "Bruce was the one gettin' stabbed."

"No." Connie covered her mouth. "Bruce? Stabbed? Wait, proverbially, or actually?"

"He's dead, Connie!" Marlene burst into tears and hung herself on Connie's shoulders. She sobbed. "They're coming after me next," she bawled. "Unless—"

"Unless?" Connie pushed Marlene gently away by the shoulders so she could look at her friend's face.

"I'm so sorry, Connie," she whispered, spittle and snot flying from her lips. "I didn't know what else to say."

"What did you say, then?" Connie asked.

"I heard them talking about buying an old abandoned building—a house—for their...their...oh, you know, illicit activities."

Connie kept her mouth shut, waiting for Marlene to finish.

"Bu-bu-but they think maybe the house is haunted. So

I told them I knew a gal, a real good one, who could read things."

Connie could barely understand Marlene through her crying, but she got enough to know to shove her friend away from her in shock. She closed her eyes and tried to remain calm. Surely there was a way out of this. Read things, yes. An entire house?

"Who are they?" Connie asked.

Marlene whimpered and sniffled and didn't answer.

"Marlene," Connie shouted, opening her eyes. "Who are the people you swindled? Who are the people you lied to?"

Marlene let out a little squeak. "David Dupont."

The world shifted and seemed to rush at her and away at the same time. "David Dupont, as in *the* David Dupont. As in the biggest drug trafficker, mob boss, top dog, whatever in the city?" Connie's voice became shrill at the end of her question.

Marlene nodded, tear-filled eyes peeking out above her hands clasped over the lower half of her face.

"You stupid—" Connie paced back and forth, then stopped in front of Marlene. "And you told him I could read a *whole house*?"

Marlene nodded again.

Connie looked at her hands. Since her mother passed, her ability to read had been enough to get by, but it had definitely lessened. She reached for Marlene to grab her by the shoulders to shake her, to rattle her stupid little brain inside her stupid little skull. Before she could, Marlene dropped the last straw on Connie's camel's back.

"He'll pay you. A lot," she blurted. "I mean a lot. I

mean, no more performing."

"It sounds like there's a *but* in there, Marlene."

She looked down at the ground. "But only if the place has good vibes. Only if he can buy it...safely." She flicked her eyes back up to Connie's.

"Okay, easy enough. I walk in, walk around, touch things, gasp, ooh aaah, come out and tell him it's fine. Easy money, right?"

Marlene swallowed so hard she had to lift her chin to get the knot out of her throat. "You have to spend the night."

Connie furrowed her brow. "Okay, so?"

Marlene took a deep breath. "It's the old Fairgrieve mansion. You know, the one that's been abandoned for seven years? The one that every new tenant moves in with dreams to renovate and remodel ends up—you know—"

"Dead." Connie finished for her.

Marlene wrung her hands in their little lace tea gloves.

It still sounded like easy money. Sleep in an old building all night, come out, tell the bloke it was fine and dandy, get some money. The question was—

"How much will I get?" Connie asked. "How much is this job worth?"

"You would have enough to buy a place. Open your shop. Stock it with all your mystical trinkets and such." Marlene gave her the exact figure.

Her friend was right. It was retire-off-the-streets money. It was money that would have paid off the bank, the creditors, bought a nice casket, and she still would have had enough left over for Connie to live comfortably for a time. Plus open the shop.

She didn't want dollar signs to cha-ching in her eyes, but they did. She'd had enough of this. Her mom's sad funeral, her evil sister, the idiot who beat women and laughed about it.

"I'll do it," Connie said. "I'll do it, but damn you, Marlene, you need to stay out of trouble. And you need to not get me involved in your trouble if you can't stay out of it."

Maybe she'd use some of the money to help Marlene, or give Marlene a job in the shop to get her off the street. Connie knew Marlene's other job was far less savory than working in a laundromat. It's how she got involved with Bruce in the first place.

"I'm sorry about Bruce," Connie said in a softer voice. Marlene's face crumpled.

Connie and Marlene met at the old Fairgrieve mansion off of Winchester and Argyle. The monstrosity and its grounds took up an entire block by itself, sitting all dismal and dreary on its own.

Because of the stories surrounding this place, her blood chilled at the thought of stepping one toe inside.

A shiny black car pulled up. One of David Dupont's flunkies got out of the passenger seat and moved around to the back door. He opened it up, and when he turned, Connie saw it was the man. The button man who'd pissed his pants.

"You—" She started forward, but Marlene caught her arm and held her back.

"Don't make any sudden moves," she said. "Don't say anything unless he talks to you."

Connie bit her lips. The pants-pisser smirked at her.

David Dupont's shiny shoes were the first thing Connie saw. Then the top of his blond head. Sunglasses obscured his eyes. She didn't like not being able to see someone's eyes. To her relief, he removed the sunglasses and slid them into the pocket of his blue sport coat. He smiled at Connie. A smile that could light a mine shaft a mile under the ground, except this smile held so much darkness, Connie wasn't really sure if it could.

"You must be Connie." His rich voice rumbled out of his mouth. He held out a hand.

Connie eyed the hand as he stepped closer to her. Marlene nudged her with her shoulder. Connie held her own out, and Dupont took it, twisting her hand so his was on top. Connie countered this power move by placing her other hand on top of his.

"So nice to meet you," she said with a gritted-teeth smile. She patted his hand, gave it a squeeze.

He met her eyes, crinkled his with a knowing smirk, and nodded.

"The deal is simple," he said, buttoning his suit jacket while looking up at the house's exterior. It really was a stunning domicile. Three stories tall, maybe more if it had a basement, which Connie was sure it must. Wings spread out on either side of it. She had seen pictures of it before, in the paper, when a new prospect purchased it. She knew the wings circled the block and enclosed a lush but overgrown garden, complete with an algae-swamped swimming pool.

What secrets lay within? she wondered.

"Connie," Marlene hissed.

Connie looked at her, then at Dupont, who seemed to be waiting impatiently.

"Now that I have your attention," he said. "The deal, as I said, is simple. Go in, spend the night, read the house, tell me if it's—"

"Haunted?" Connie finished.

Dupont laughed. It was the sound of patience wearing thin, like she was an ignorant child who asked a stupid question she should know the answer to.

"Let me make one thing clear," he said, thumbing his nose. He stared into her. "I don't believe in ghosts." He clasped his hands behind his back and paced away from her. "I need to make sure this house is...safe." He eyed her.

"Safe? For what?" Connie asked.

Dupont gave her a sharp look.

Connie shrugged. "I need to know the details, sir, in order to tell you if it's safe. Safe for a child to run around barefoot is different than safe for your pants-pissing associate—"

"Hey—" The pants-pisser stepped forward.

Dupont held him back with a hand to the brawny man's chest.

"Safe for my associate, here," he said in that low silken voice. "That's all you need to know."

Connie narrowed her eyes at the pants-pisser. She raised an eyebrow at him and nodded. "Spend the night, read the house. Got it." She turned to the front of the house and climbed the stone steps leading up to the massive front doors.

Connie took a deep breath, sure she wouldn't be able to

read a thing inside this house. Not without her mother there to amplify her ability. It didn't matter. All she had to do was spend the night, come out in the morning, tell him it was fine...he hadn't mentioned anything about details. Even if he asked, she could make things up.

She heaved the front door open and stepped inside.

Chaos filled her mind. It flung itself at her from all directions. She didn't see through her eyes, but through her sight. Everything jumped around, glitchy, grainy, streaked with age. Disoriented, she flung out a hand, grabbed nothing, and fell to her hands and knees.

Up on the second-floor landing, a beefy figure in a butcher's apron dragged a giant sledge hammer behind him. The side of his face was caved in. A woman sobbed black tears from a doorway to her right. She moved her hands from her face, and her eyes sat glistening in her palms.

At the end of the hall, a child sat cross-legged, back to her, hands busy doing something. Wet noises came from that direction.

The figures she could see weren't the worst of it, disturbing as they were. It was the sounds that threatened to break her.

Under a near-deafening roar, children sang "Ring Around the Rosy" from somewhere in a sickeningly slow cadence. It echoed all around.

Deep inside the cacophony, a woman laughed shrieking laughter that turned into wailing sobs and back into choked wet giggles.

Connie wanted to get the hell out of this place of madness, but when she turned around, the door she had entered was gone. The house she had entered was gone. A bleak blackness spread out before her, as if the edge of the house had been shorn off by a guillotine. She reached a hand into the dark. It disappeared, and she jerked back by the abrupt and icy cold inside.

She backed away from that inky black.

A hand gripped her shoulder. She spun around, confronted by the face of the woman with no eyes, just dark pits in her face where they should be. Veins of the same color crackled out from the edges of those empty holes. The woman opened her mouth and screamed.

Connie covered her ears and dropped to a crouch, tucking her face between her knees, making herself as small as possible. She closed her eyes and willed the sounds to stop.

"Help," someone whispered.

Connie wasn't sure how she heard it. Even with her ears covered, the symphony of terror assaulted her.

And then silence so abrupt, Connie thought she'd gone deaf. Even the constant rush from her tinnitus vanished.

"Help."

Connie lifted her head and opened her eyes.

They stood in a circle around her, the makers of the sounds. The children who sang, the woman who screamed, the butcher with the overlarge hammer. And others. So many others.

"Help." A woman right in front of Connie mouthed the whispered word.

Connie gasped and covered her mouth.

Her mother stepped forward, holding out her cupped hands. Her favorite necklace lay inside her palms.

"Mom," Connie's voice whispered out of her choked

throat. She held out her hands. Her mom opened her own and dropped the necklace into Connie's open palms.

Connie's ears popped and all the figures vanished. The crash of objects hitting the floor where they'd just been standing forced her to cover her ears and close her eyes. Clattering, crashing. Silence again.

She opened her eyes and lowered her hands from her ears. All around her lay items and objects. Trinkets small enough to be concealed on bodies.

She lifted her mother's necklace, held it to her chest, and learned the truth.

When Connie stepped out of the house into the thin dawning light, exhaustion made her stumble on the steps. Marlene caught her by her elbows.

"Are you okay? You look like you went through hell and back."

Connie squeezed Marlene's hand and nodded. She *had* been through hell and back. She'd spent the night reading every object left by every victim. She'd gathered them into the pockets of her dress, concealed them in her bodice. All those souls trapped inside that house because of one man.

The pants-pisser.

"Is it safe?" Dupont asked.

Connie flicked her eyes to the other man, leaning against the car with a nervous smirk on his face. "Yes," she said, meeting his eyes. "It's perfectly safe."

Tommy's Teeth

BOX OF TEETH

My mother had a hope chest at the end of her bed. It was forbidden for us to look inside, which, of course, made it that much more desirable.

We could always tell when Mama wore a shirt or skirt or shawl from the chest. It had a certain smell. A musty smell, tinged with the spicy scent of cedar. And something else we weren't sure of. We couldn't tell if it was a good smell or a bad one. It was one of those smells you need to take another whiff, just to see if you can figure it out.

She kept her bedroom locked, and if the door was open, it meant she was in there. There was no way for us to sneak in and peek inside that forbidden chest.

But one day, our little brother Tommy had an *amazing* idea. He was full of mischief and often had *ideas* he thought were great, but almost always got us all in trouble with Mama.

There were three of us. I was the middle child by seven minutes.

Now...I'm the youngest.

Tommy's idea seemed sound. It wasn't laced with delusions of grandeur like some of his other ideas. The thing with Tommy was, even if Lola and I refused to go along with his plans, he threatened to dish our secrets—of which he had many, being the snoopy and nosy little brother he was—to Mama. We had to go along with his plans. Besides, he really did have a way of manipulating us. He was very charismatic and handed out guilt trips like candy to kids at a parade.

"Sandy," he whispered to me. "I know how we can look in the chest."

I knew from the gleam in his eyes we would carry out this plan no matter what, because that gleam always meant he got what he wanted.

"Go on, tell me your plan." I put down the book I was reading and gave him my attention.

"The next time Mama's in her room and the door is open, I'll pretend to be injured. I'll cry out. You or Lola, probably you because you're the tattliest tattle taler—" He held up his hands when my mouth popped open to retort. "Just stating facts, sis."

"Fine," I muttered. "Go on."

"You'll run in and tell Mama something bad happened to me."

"What happened to you?" I asked.

Tommy shrugged. "You'll have to come up with something good."

I hated when he did this. It was his way of coercing me into fully immersing myself in his plan. If I had to come up with something, it meant I was part of the scheming, which means I'm more than just a witness being fed lines, or a bystander caught up in the angry mob. It means I'm an accomplice.

"Mama won't have time to lock the door," Tommy said, the gleam in his eye sparkling again. He rubbed his hands together in an overly dramatic, evil villain kind of way. If only he had a mustache to twirl.

All the doors in our house locked using skeleton keys, like in the movie *The Others*. Mama kept the key to her room with her at all times on a string around her neck, but the rest of them were on a keyring in the top drawer of the roll-top desk in a room we called the parlor. We knew this because we'd searched for them one time, found them, and tried every single one on her bedroom door to no avail.

"I thought all skeleton keys opened all skeleton keyholes," Tommy had said.

"Me too," Lola and I both had said at the same time, as we often did, being twins and all.

Tommy nodded. I could hear him thinking, *Yes, this plan is perfect. Nothing will go wrong. Nothing at all.*

"While Mama is off to find me, you and Lola can sneak into her room, open the chest, and take pictures of what's inside. Or steal something out of there, rummage, figure out why it's so secret." He shrugged. "Then you can tell me what you saw or show me the pictures or whatever after. When I'm *safely* back in the house." He nodded the entire time he said the plan. I found I was nodding along with him. A sneaky tactic.

I had to admit, though. The plan was kind of brilliant.

Tommy wanted a week to really prepare. He knew I'd need time to work out what I would say when I ran in all panicky and shrieky.

We didn't have to wait that long, though, and we didn't have to make anything up.

While out in the woods surrounding our house, I went beyond the barrier of our lot. Mama told us to not go past our fence, but I traveled our whole property in a grid pattern and didn't find any inspiration for what could *happen* to Tommy.

Using our huge climbing tree, I climbed onto a lower branch and dropped over the six-foot fence.

A bleak landscape greeted me. I shielded my eyes from the sun, which had been blocked by all the trees. Tall golden grass swayed in an unfelt breeze.

I picked my way through the grass, and not too far in, I found a hole in the ground.

Not a hole like a gopher or prairie dog dug, but a big hole. Deep—I couldn't see the bottom. Like someone had drilled there with a five-foot-diameter drill bit. I carefully picked my way a little farther into the field and found another one. I ran back to our property line and hoisted myself up and over the fence with the assistance of a branch hanging down. I climbed higher into the huge tree. I'd climbed this tree so many times before, but this time, I looked out over the field and saw the land riddled with these holes.

I didn't know what they were, but maybe someone had been drilling for oil or water for a well or something? They must not have found it, because that lot is still vacant even to this day.

I scrambled down the tree and ran inside, collected Tommy and Lola and brought them to the fence.

"Here's the story, Morning Glories," I said. "Tommy, being the little scamp he is, decides to climb the fence to check out the vacant lot—"

"Hold on," Tommy interrupted. "Mama's gonna be pissed if you tell her that."

"Exactly." I crossed my arms and lifted my chin. "It's forbidden, right? She learns you're over there, she'll come running straightaway."

Tommy grinned and nodded.

"Why do you think she wants us to stay out of that lot?" I asked them.

Tommy looked at Lola. Lola looked at Tommy. They both shrugged and looked at me.

"I know why. Follow me." We went to the climbing tree and climbed up as high as Lola was brave enough to go, which was just high enough to see over the fence—she wasn't as daring as Tommy and me ever since that time she climbed too high and couldn't get back down.

I spotted one of the holes and pointed to it.

"This field has probably a hundred of those big holes."

"What holes?" Lola asked, squinting. I put my face next to hers so our eyes were together and pointed. "Oh."

"They're about five feet wide and I don't even know how deep."

Tommy stared out over the field, a ponderous look in his eyes. "I climbed the fence into the vacant lot," he said with wonder. "And I—what?—fell in a hole?"

I nodded.

He shook his head. "I don't know. If those holes are as big as you say they are, I'd see it before I fell in."

"The grass is super tall," I said.

"Let's look." Tommy used the same branch I did and climbed down. Lola and I followed.

I didn't know if Lola and Tommy had ever been on the other side of the fence, but they both landed and let out whooshing breaths, as if they thought we were on another planet and wouldn't be able to breathe.

"Follow me," I said. I could see the path where I'd tramped down the grass when I was out here before scouting the area. At the end of the path was the first hole I'd found. "Here it is."

Tommy leaned out. I grabbed the back of his shirt and he flung his arms wildly, maybe thinking I was going to push him in. One of his hands caught me under the chin and clapped my trap shut hard. I bit my tongue and let go of his shirt to grab my face.

Tommy let out a sound halfway between a *whoa* and a grunt. Lola screamed. Tommy disappeared into the hole.

A few seconds passed before I realized what had happened. Lola was already over the fence screaming for Mama.

"Tommy?" I shrieked, dropping to my hands and knees and leaning over the dark hole. A hand darted out of the darkness and grabbed the front of my shirt. It pulled me in. I didn't even have time to cry out.

Laughter filled the darkness. Tommy's laughter. I looked up. The edge of the hole was right above my head.

"It's some sort of illusion, I think," he said.

We stood in the bottom of the hole. The opening was

only about a foot above our heads, but from the outside of it, pure darkness.

"Even if Lola comes back with Mama, she won't be able to see us." I said. "I couldn't see you at all from out there. It was like this hole was miles deep."

Tommy scratched his head, thinking. He pulled his hand away, looked at it, and flipped it like something was stuck to his fingers. He touched his head again.

"Is there blood here?" he asked me.

"I can't tell. Let's get out of here. It's creeping me out."

We climbed out of the hole, and I looked at Tommy with a gasp. His black hair, coveted by Lola and me—we both had mouse-brown hair—had turned yellow.

"What?" he asked, reaching for his hair.

"Nothing," I said. "Nothing. Let me see your head." He tilted his chin down.

There was blood there, right in the middle of a bald patch, like that small section of his head had been scalped. I parted his hair more to see better and chunks of it came off in my fingertips, leaving more bald patches.

"Oh my God," I whispered.

"What? Is it bad?" He turned his eyes to me. The whites were bloodshot. His skin held a deathly pallor. A sickly grayness tinged with green.

"Tommy!" Mama shrieked as she flung herself over the fence with such animal grace, it replays in my mind randomly to this day. "Oh God, Tommy!" She ran to us. "Oh God, no." She dropped to her knees and pulled him against her. On her knees, her cheek pressed against his belly. She groped for my hand and scratched my arm.

"Mama, what's wrong with him?" I asked in a shocked whisper. Faint red lines spider-webbed his gray-green skin.

Lola bawled a few feet away, head thrown back, mouth agape, face red. "Tah-ah-ah-ah-meeeee!"

"What? What's wrong with me?" Tommy asked. He pulled away from her and looked at his hands, at the gray flesh there.

"We have to get away from this place. Come on." She pulled us by our arms. Lola walked ahead of us, stumbling and crying. You'd have thought *she* was the youngest.

Mama surprised us by opening a hatch in the fence not too far from where we climbed over. We ducked under. I avoided looking at him. At that sickly pallor. The way his skin drooped.

Mama left Lola and me in the woods by the fence and rushed Tommy to the house.

"What was wrong with him, Sandy? Why did he look like that?"

"I don't know." I grabbed her hand and pulled her through the woods to the house. We burst inside.

Mama was on the floor cradling Tommy's limp form in her arms, head tossed back to the heavens, keening.

Lola's sobs erupted from her, renewed, joining Mama's wails. I stared at that still form. At the way his arm stuck straight out, his wrist loose. The way his hand flopped with each movement Mama made. I fixated on that.

"Why why why," Mama cried. "Not another one, please, why."

I looked at Lola, but her bawling probably drowned out Mama's words in her ears.

Not another one.

It was then I noticed the door to her bedroom stood open.

Maybe I was in shock. I'd been in that hole, too. Maybe whatever got Tommy would get me, too, and if it was going to, I had to know what was in that trunk before it took me.

For Tommy.

As I moved past Mama—blind to anything outside of the world of desperate anguish she lived in now—I tugged at my hair. It didn't come out in chunks. It was strong and attached.

In her room, I quietly and carefully lifted the lid of the cedar hope chest. The scent of the wood wafted out first. A comforting spicy scent. Then that musty smell tinged with that other, strange, unknown and unknowable smell.

Skirts, dresses, shawls, blouses neatly folded sat on top. A few items I'd seen Mama wear, but not often. I moved them all aside.

Underneath were a handful of small yellow boxes. I leaned in to pick one up, that sickly sweet smell growing stronger. The box rattled when I lifted it.

It was the kind of box in which the lid fits snug over the base. I worked to slide it out, rattling the contents with each movement to get that lid off. Finally, it slid free.

The smell intensified. I looked inside.

The teeth lay on a layer of cotton batting. Despite their careful packaging, a few had fallen beneath it—hence the rattling. They were perfectly white except the roots, tinged with old browned blood.

I dropped it. It hit the rug, and the teeth scattered.

Not another one.

I looked at the lid, still in my hand. Scrawled in Mama's

neat handwriting was *Tommy II* followed by a date. A date from long before Lola and I were born.

Not another one.

I looked back into the depths of the hope chest, all hope lost. I pushed blankets and more clothing aside.

There were seven boxes. I reached in and got the lids off of three of the boxes—all scrawled with Tommy, a number, and a date—before Mama stopped me. By then I was screaming, too. Screaming and tearing at the boxes. When Mama grabbed me, I tore at her hands and arms. She wrestled me to the ground and pressed my face against her bosom, shushing me and petting my hair.

My hair that wasn't falling out in chunks. I swiveled my eyes and found Lola huddled in the corner with her thumb in her mouth. She hadn't sucked her thumb in five years, since we were six.

"Sandy, Sandy," Mama cooed. "Sandy, it's okay."

I struggled out of her arms. "It's not okay, Mama! It's not okay!" I ran out of her room. I didn't want to look at Tommy's body, but I couldn't help it. The smell. It was that smell from the hope chest. The one we could never identify.

Tommy's body was no longer a body, but a gelatinous blob in the center of a brownish Tommy-shaped puddle. At the head of the puddle were teeth. Tommy's perfectly white teeth.

"I can explain, please, girls. Let me explain."

I didn't let her explain at first. I ran out of the house. After a few hours sitting in the branches of the climbing tree, she came out to find me.

"Sandy, come inside. It's getting chilly out."

She was right. I'd been shivering from my perch for at least half an hour.

I climbed down and she tucked me under her arm. "Lola's okay," she said. "I explained everything to her already."

I said nothing. I'd been closer to Tommy than Lola was. She was always off in her own world, and he and I were the ones who plotted and planned and schemed together. She was the innocent bystander swept up in the mob. The witness fed lines.

"Why didn't I get sick like him?" Guilt trickled into my belly and churned there. It should have been me. Tommy had so much more going for him than I ever did. Good in school, charismatic, a handsome little devil.

"The holes in the field," Mama started. She swallowed hard. "They once held barrels of unidentifiable toxic waste. No one knows where they came from. For a time the government thought it was the Soviets, then the Chinese, then aliens."

I snorted. It was a scoffing sound. I thought she was joking and now was not the time to joke. Not with Tommy...gone.

"I'm serious, Sandra."

"Oh."

"I was part of the team that came in to clean up the site. Each barrel was marked with T0-M1. We thought maybe it was some sort of a chemical compound from wherever the barrels came from. Regardless." She waved her hand to dismiss it. "T0-M1 became Tommy. The project became known as the Tommy Project." She sniffled, lifted a hand to her face and wiped away a tear. "Each barrel had a Tommy inside."

"Wait...what?" I couldn't have heard her right, but she kept on talking.

"The beings inside the barrels, coated in some sort of material that protected them from the toxic waste that filled the empty space inside the barrels, activated when cut out of the packaging."

I stopped. "They came alive?"

Mama nodded. Tears glistened in her eyes. "They were children. Boys. Human in every way, except...when they got near the holes or the chemicals in the barrels, they—" She flung a hand toward the house and didn't have to say more.

They melted.

"How did you go through seven—" I closed my eyes and gulped. "Eight," I whispered. "Tommys."

"They're drawn to the holes for some reason we never figured out. But the trace amounts of toxic waste left are detrimental." Her face crumbled with a sob. I wrapped my arms around her.

"I wasn't supposed to have them," Mama whispered into the top of my head. "But the government was going to destroy them. I couldn't let them do that. This was a long time ago. Your father and I had tried to have children, but we couldn't." She spoke fast.

"But you had Lola and me."

Her voice softened, and she looked down at me, caressed my cheek. "Yes. I was blessed with two beautiful babies at once, thanks to modern reproductive medicine."

We started walking to the house again. "The Tommys

were going to be destroyed, and in my eyes, it was our only chance at having a child, back then, I mean.

"After the second Tommy succumbed to his desire to look at the holes, your father left. He couldn't take it. I didn't tell Lola this part. I don't think she would take it as easily, but you, Sandy. You are wise beyond your years. So mature sometimes." She held my hand now. "You kept good care of Tommy."

Now I cried. It was my fault Tommy was a pile of teeth in our living room. I found the holes. I grabbed him and made him fall in. I might as well have pushed him.

I didn't tell her it was my fault. That was a shameful, guilty secret I'd carry to my grave.

"I thought this one would keep forever," she whispered, gazing up at the stars. "He was the last one of his kind."

I couldn't sleep that night. I kept seeing Tommy's bloodied scalp. Chunks of hair. His skin. The pile of teeth. Every time I closed my eyes, it was a different thing cycling through on repeat like a View-Master reel. I wept quietly and cursed myself for having found the holes, cursed Mama for not moving away from them—why stay if all the Tommys died because of them? I cursed my unknown father for allowing her to keep them.

Lola slept soundly, even when she hadn't experienced a traumatic event. I crept out of our room and snuck out the back door. I gazed up at the stars.

I missed Tommy. I missed him so much it hurt my lungs. I would never see that gleam in his eye again, or wonder what fresh hell he was going to put us through to carry out his next amazing idea.

I walked to the climbing tree and climbed up to the

branch we'd all perched on to look at the holes. I don't know how long I was there, but a sound below me shook me out of a light sleep. Luckily, I'd leaned back against the trunk and hadn't fallen.

"Who's there?" I whispered into the dark, thinking it was Lola, or maybe Mama, coming to find me.

Scratch, scratch, scratch.

I climbed down, senses on high alert. Eyes wide, ears pricked.

The moonlight gleamed off a head of black hair, and I knew Mama lied to me when she said he'd been the last one.

"Tommy?" My heart beat in my throat. My eyes prickled and my nose burned in the way of tears. "Tommy?"

He stopped scratching at the fence and looked at me. I stepped closer, holding my hand out. I touched his arm and he didn't move. I took his hand.

"Tommy?" I whispered.

He swiped his other hand across his nose. I laughed. I whooped. I pulled him into my arms, even though I knew it wasn't *my* Tommy. He could become my Tommy, couldn't he?

I sniffled and exhaled and laughed. A piece of his hair sucked in and out of my nose. I held him at arm's length, taking in his face—his very *Tommy* face—and pulled him back against me.

I would tell him all about the fun times we'd had together—number eight and I. All the mischief. I'd fill him in, and it would be just like he never went in that hole and—

Sticks broke. Leaves rustled. More Tommys came out of the darkness and into the moonlight, drawn to the holes.

I stared around at them.

The Tommy still in my arms pulled gently away. I let him go, but he didn't turn away. The moonlight shone on his black hair. His eyes gleamed. He cocked his head and leaned in.

"I have an amazing idea," he said.

Amelia's Monster Part 1: Secrets and All

THE SENTENCE THAT CHANGED EVERYTHING

Amelia was in the grocery store parking lot when she received the call. The number was from her hometown—Fairhaven. The man identified himself as Detective Something.

"We found your mother," he said.

Amelia gripped her phone with both hands. She hadn't even known her mother was missing. Why would she know? Amelia hadn't spoken to her in over a decade.

"I mean, we think we found her." He cleared his throat. "I mean, Chantel Langland is your mother? Is this—" Pause. Throat clear. "—Amelia Langland?"

Amelia made an affirmative sound, afraid her actual voice would fail her.

Found implied missing. Missing implied kidnapping, or maybe wandering off. "Is she okay?" Had Mom's mind deteriorated like Grandma's had?

"The body we discovered on her property was disfigured by a wild animal."

"Body?" Amelia's voice squeaked. She gripped her seat belt, suddenly too tight, across her chest.

Amelia heard the faint sound of another throat clearing. "Something with...teeth...and claws. We need you to come and—" He cleared his throat *again*.

Amelia was about to recommend a lozenge or a drink of water, but his next words cut her off.

"Identify the body."

"I'm sorry, what?" Amelia wasn't sure she heard him right, distracted as she was by his throat clearing and the clinical tone of his voice delivering this unexpected message.

"We need you to come to town—I'm assuming by your phone number you aren't *in* town—to identify the body. You're her only next of kin. You *are* her daughter, right?"

He'd mentioned teeth and claws. "Is there enough left to..." now *she* cleared *her* throat, "identify it?"

"Did your mother have any identifiable marks on her body? Moles, tattoos, anything like that?"

A single tear slithered from Amelia's eye. She wiped it away, not sure why she cried. Was it all the years between them? Was it the monster her mother had become over the years before Amelia left? Was it relief? She didn't know.

"Yes. She had a tattoo on the inside of her wrist. I'll come right away." Fairhaven was only a few hours away. She could get there before sundown.

After ending the call, Amelia drove home, hastily shoved all of her groceries into the fridge whether they needed refrigeration or not, packed a bag, and threw it into the trunk of her car. She peered in the rearview mirror to back out of the driveway. A storm loomed in the distance. She'd be heading right into it.

We found your mother.

The detective's voice echoed through her mind. She didn't realize phrases could get stuck in a person's head. Like a song. Like a chant.

Teeth...and claws. We found your mother. Teeth...and claws. We found your mother.

Amelia pictured the house in her mind while she drove. It was one of those Victorian models people always gushed about. Amelia had hated living there. It had been a relic among modern cookie-cutter homes. As if that wasn't bad enough, it perched on top of a hill at the end of a cul-de-sac. The driveway wound up the side of the hill.

It was *that* house. The one the neighborhood kids made up stories about. Witches, vampires, cannibals. Amelia wasn't any of those things, but living in that house made her fellow schoolmates tease and taunt her.

She was the weirdo who lived in Shirley Jackson's Hill House.

The house itself wasn't scary. The exterior was white, not gray, or some other drab color. The gingerbread trim was a piggy-pink color. It kind of looked like a wedding cake, to be honest.

Inside, there were very few dark corners, because every room had windows. When she finally made friends and brought them to her humble home, the bright and cheery interior disappointed them. They wanted it to be haunted.

To Amelia, it *was* haunted.

Those kids didn't know the house's secrets. The scars.

Could a house become haunted by the memories that lived inside its walls? Amelia wondered.

If her mom was lying in the morgue, what would Amelia *do* with the house?

She would sell it. That was for certain. She wouldn't live there. She didn't even want to set foot inside. She could sell it as is, furnishings and all.

Scars and all.

Secrets and all.

But a part of her—some morbidly curious part—had to go back in. Had to see for herself. Because the one room she remembered the most, that held the most scars, was not her bedroom. It wasn't the creepy walk-up attic either. Nor the basement proper. It was the laundry room.

The laundry room was in the basement at the bottom of a set of creaking wooden stairs. Spiders took up residence in the exposed ceiling beams. Strange wet sounds constantly issued from the drain in the middle of the sinking floor. The single bulb, operated by a pull cord, of course, always swung, throwing shadows around where shadows ought not to be.

If her mother forgot to do the laundry earlier in the week, Amelia would venture to the laundry room, arms laden with a basket of dirty clothes. She always paused at the top of the creaking stairs, took a deep breath, and closed her eyes. She counted each step. At the bottom, she took three long strides, put the basket on her hip and gripped the string overhead. She gave it a sharp jerk.

If the laundry room door was open, it was a gaping, ominous hole. The bare bulb didn't reach into that space. There was another pull cord inside. Another bare bulb.

The laundry room held the washer and dryer, the boiler

that always made weird sounds, and the hole in the wall near the floor by the washing machine.

Noises came from that hole. Scratching sounds. Wet sounds. Sloppy sounds.

Water in the pipes, rats in the walls, Amelia told herself now, remembering that terrible room. *My own wet sobs and snot-filled sniffles.*

When Amelia was five years old, her mother had told her a story about a monster that lived in the laundry room. The monster was a constant threat to Amelia's safety. She had better behave or it would come and get her.

It was a typical tale told to frighten children into obedience. The monster would steal bad kids in the middle of the night and drag them kicking and screaming to its den inside that gap near the floor by the washing machine, where it would snack on their bones and flesh. Her mother always used the word flesh, and the way she said it— chardonnay threatening to slosh out of her wine glass— always gave Amelia chills. Oh, how her mom's eyes gleamed with excitement at frightening her only child.

Amelia found herself pulling up to the bottom of the porch steps at her mom's house. Her childhood home. She hadn't meant to go straight to the house, but muscle memory took over while the past filled her mind.

On this side of the storm, the skies were clear, bright, cheery.

The house loomed above her, as old Victorian houses are wont to do. If it hadn't been a nice day, she would have expected a lightning bolt and a loud clap of thunder. That's the kind of house it was.

Amelia didn't drink, but if she did, she would have

brought a flask, taken a long pull from it, and climbed out like a detective from Bogart's days.

She should go to the station, identify the—

Teeth...and claws. We found your mother.

Amelia took a deep breath and climbed out of her car.

The house had one of those grand entryways with a wide staircase climbing to the second floor, and hallways and doorways branching in every direction. As Amelia peered around the house she'd grown up in, more memories flitted and flickered to life in the streaming sunbeams.

She and her mom danced into the living room, feather dusters in hand, pretending to be fairies cleaning the massive place before the princess awoke to find them keeping things tidy. In the dining room, they pretended to be royalty, shouting down the nine-foot table to please pass the salt, then sliding it as far down the length of the polished wood as they could before laughing and getting up to retrieve it from the middle.

These memories should have made her smile, but they didn't. Because the more recent memories cast dark shadows over Amelia's life.

Mom's good days became few and far between.

Amelia pretended to be the lone fairy dumping empty wine bottles into the recycling bin night after night while her mother snored on the couch in the living room.

Tiptoe through the dead soldiers.

One time, she tripped and the wine bottles smashed and clattered onto the hardwood. Her mother woke.

Noisy Nellies need to learn their lessons. Her mom's disheveled hair and smeared makeup turned her into a monster herself. With what seemed like abnormal strength, her mom dragged Amelia down the basement stairs and flung her inside the laundry room, slamming the door behind her. It was the first time Amelia was locked in the scary little room.

Amelia scrambled for the pull string to turn on the bare bulb while the boiler hissed and burbled and scratching sounds echoed from deep inside that gap in the wall near the washing machine.

Breaths heaving, spraying snot and spittle from her nose and mouth, the cord hit her fingers. She tugged it. The light came on. Amelia cowered as far away from that corner as she could, waiting for the monster to come out. Hearing it scratching and scrambling against the gravel inside. A few loose rocks had tumbled outside the hovel, as if the creature had dug that hole deeper to live in, to wait in, to devour her flesh in.

She curled into a ball and covered her head, making herself as small as possible, face contorted in silent frightened bawling. She dare not look at that gap despite the noises coming from it. If she *saw* the creature, it would become real.

After some indeterminate amount of time, her mother would open the door and Amelia would scramble out. Sometimes her mom would give her a hug and tell her she was sorry. Other times, Mom only looked at her with an expressionless face and point to the stairs. Her mom would gaze into the laundry room for a time, seemingly disappointed that Amelia was still alive, still covered in her intact flesh, before turning and following Amelia up the stairs.

Now, still in the grand entryway, Amelia gazed around,

trying not to feel the memories. She went from room to room and they washed over her. Good days followed by bad days in each one. Good days when they'd first moved in. When living in such a grand house had been exciting. Something she and her widowed mother had dreamed of. Then the bad ones. Amelia was a little older. The playful mother she'd known dissipating day by day.

Fairies, fancy ladies, royalty.

Irritation, anger, disappointment.

Good memory, bad memory, worse memory.

In the dining room, Amelia slid the salt shaker down the table. It left a clean trail in the thick layer of dust before coming to a stop.

No fairies to clean up after I left.

Up on the second floor, the floorboards creaked in all the places she remembered. Places she'd memorized so she could sneak out as a teenager to meet up with Kate, her best friend. Kate was the only one who knew about Amelia's mother's unpredictable moods and flip-floppy personality. Kate always greeted Amelia at school with three words: good or bad? "Good" meant Amelia hadn't spent time in the laundry room the night before.

Kate told Amelia she should get emancipated and get away from that woman. Kate herself, who had an abusive father, had done that. She moved away at sixteen. She'd desperately wanted Amelia to come with her. They could make a life together. Amelia still didn't know why she hadn't.

It was the time before cell phones when long distance still cost money, and email wasn't really a thing yet. They wrote letters. Kate sent her trinkets and other things through the mail. Amelia responded in kind at first, but soon the weekly letters and packages became monthly, became every once in a while—a card on her birthday. A card for Christmas—then nothing.

Amelia went to her old room. It was just as she'd left it when she moved out after high school graduation.

Mom had been having a good day that day, which made it really hard for Amelia to leave. They laughed. They had champagne from actual France even though Amelia was only eighteen. They reminisced about the fairies, fancy ladies, royalty. For half a second, her mother's face took on a distant quality, almost as if she were peering into her regrets. Then she shook herself and smiled at Amelia.

"This bubbly's gone straight to my head. I think I'll go lie down."

Amelia heard her mother's wet sniffles as she took the bottle up the stairs with her. Full of guilt, choking on tears, Amelia left in the middle of the night. She vowed she would never return to this place.

Yet here she was.

In her old room.

Untouched since she left and therefore extra dusty.

From under her bed, she pulled out an old shoebox, fighting with spider webs and dust bunnies to dislodge it from the floor. It was full of Kate's letters and trinkets and origami.

She spent too much time reading the letters, avoiding the inevitable. It was a feeling inside her head. A pressure behind her eyes. A ringing in her ears.

Even though the thought of clopping down those rickety stairs filled her with dread, she knew she had to look.

That little room had haunted Amelia her entire life. She still woke in the dead of night, having visited that room in her nightmares, tears of fear trapped under her eyelids.

She tucked Kate's letters and trinkets back in the box and stood. After dusting off the seat of her pants, she took determined steps out of the room and back down to the bottom of the grand staircase. Each step added another stone to her gut.

She went to the walk-in pantry. Inside was the door to the basement.

Amelia touched the doorknob on the door that would open into darkness. She turned and scanned the pantry shelves, found a flashlight, tested it.

The light flicked on. It was a dull warm glow of an old flashlight, not the blindingly bright LED like the ones she had at home.

"It'll do. I guess."

She opened the door. The darkness confronted her like an impenetrable mass. The dull glow from the flashlight did nothing to dispel it. Amelia closed her eyes and took the first step onto those wooden stairs.

At the bottom. She took measured steps forward, hand held aloft until the pull cord hit her palm. The single bulb revealed the gaping mouth of the laundry room doorway. The door hung haphazardly on one hinge.

Amelia's breath burst in and out. She closed her mouth and took a deep breath through her nose, held it.

She shined the flashlight toward the dark maw. With each step, her hand shook harder and harder until she stood right inside the door frame. She leaned in, hand reaching, found the cord, tugged.

The light came to life. Amelia let out a shaking breath, but immediately sucked it back in as she took in the nightmare space from her past. Years of trauma flooded her body the moment her eyes landed on the hovel where her mother's monster lived.

As Amelia stood in the doorway of that wretched room, she realized how quiet it was.

No sounds came from that gaping hole. No burbling, no scratching sounds. Nothing.

She stood and looked at the door hanging from its single hinge. Only then did she notice the claw marks raking down the inside. The splintered wood where the latch and lock should be.

This was not the end. She had to look. She had to see.

Amelia directed the beam into the dark gap. Hands shaking—limbs shaking—Amelia crawled in after the light. She ducked under floating tails of cobwebs, loose rocks dug into her kneecaps. The light landed on a figure. Dusty and curled into itself.

With a jolt of fear, Amelia hit her head on the beam above her. She dropped the flashlight. The light still shone on the mummified figure ten feet away. Terror glued her to the floor, froze her joints, her core. It prickled over her entire body, raising every hair on her head, arms, legs.

She stared at the figure for long minutes, waiting for it to move, to uncurl, for its eyes to open and see her.

When the thing didn't move, a cold understanding came to her.

Whatever it was, it was dead. Long dead.

We found your mother.

Amelia crawled forward. Something stabbed into her

kneecap, different than just a rock. She shined the light toward her leg. Gold glinted in the dirt among the loose rocks. She lifted an earring, one of her mother's favorites, from the grime. The post was bent over where her knee smashed it. She shined the light around and snatched at every glinting object.

All of it, her mother's jewelry. She'd been so proud of her jewels. When they pretended to be royalty, they decked themselves out in these sparkling items. Family heirlooms, Mom said. Passed down through the ages.

Amelia shined the light on the curled little corpse again.

We found your mother.

She ventured forward.

We found your mother.

They hadn't found her mother.

Her mother had never left this house.

Amelia's Monster Part 2: Scars and All

GUILT

When the figure appeared in the mirror behind her, Chantel Langland whipped around with a startled gasp, prepared to laugh at her daughter, Amelia, for giving her a scare.

But no one stood behind her. She turned back to the mirror, smile gone.

In her reflection, the figure was there, right behind her. It moved with her. No matter how hard she tried to get a good look, Chantel's own reflection always blocked her view of it. She rubbed her eyes and looked again. The other person had disappeared.

Just a trick of the light or something. She dismissed it and sat in front of the vanity to do her hair and makeup.

She and Amelia had been living in the house for a few months. The vanity came with the house. Everything inside the house had belonged to the previous owner. Amelia need not know the house was *not* an inheritance from a rich aunt. That the jewels they sometimes adorned themselves with were *not* family heirlooms.

Amelia had made the assumption when she found some photos that used to hang on the walls, and Chantel went with it, making up names for the people in the photos.

"Aunt Amelia, who I named you after, and Uncle Henry." Chantel pointed at two faces who appeared frequently in the pictures.

"They're dead?" Amelia asked.

"Yes," Chantel said. "They died in a car crash." That part wasn't a lie, but saying it out loud made her throat go dry.

Amelia only needed to know what she needed to know, and that was that this house was their home, and Chantel did what she had to in order to get it for them. Luckily, "Aunt Amelia" and "Uncle Henry" had been old, and didn't have any children, and had earned disdain from their neighbors.

When Chantel and Amelia moved in, those neighbors didn't ask many questions, other than, "What happened to the old people?" and other versions that weren't so kind.

Chantel made up a story about how she was house-sitting for them while they were out of town. She went out of her way to be pleasant to everyone she encountered in the neighborhood. They all liked her and Amelia.

Thankfully, Amelia never asked about Aunt Amelia and Uncle Henry again. As it was her nature to accept what Chantel told her and move on to other, more exciting things, like playing make believe.

Amelia *loved* to play make believe. Fairies with dusters flitting from room to room, a game Chantel made up to get her to help with cleaning up the old house. At the long dining room table, they pretended to be royalty. Chantel would even bring out the previous owner's jewels. She had jewelry boxes full of necklaces, bracelets, earrings, and even hair adornments. Combs, clips, diamond-encrusted bobby pins.

But Amelia's imagination became a little too intense. She suddenly became afraid of the basement, the laundry room in particular, claiming there was a monster living in there. When pressed for where she got that idea, Amelia shook her head and bit her lips. She refused to tell Chantel anything about the monster.

While Amelia was at school one day, Chantel scoured the books in the house's library and on the shelves in Amelia's room for any stories that could have put the idea in her daughter's head. She found none.

A few months after seeing the strange figure in the mirror, Chantel woke in a daze. Headache, eyes bleary, mouth dry. On the coffee table lay two empty chardonnay bottles at odd angles on their sides.

She wasn't sure where she was, but as her vision cleared, she realized she was in the living room. She sat up, rubbing her temples, unsure of what had happened.

Did she drink all of this wine? Chantel hadn't touched the stuff since she was pregnant with Amelia six years ago. Even back when she did drink, she preferred red over white, and never a—she lifted the bottle—California chardonnay.

"Amelia?" Her voice croaked out of her parched throat. Chantel listened for her daughter's footsteps, but all she heard was the ominous *tick-tick-tick* of the grandfather clock in the grand entry.

Chantel stood, sat again when she lost her balance. Touched her forehead. This headache. She stood again, holding a hand out to steady herself against the arm of the couch. She took a step toward the doorway to call to her daughter again. Perhaps Amelia didn't hear her.

Chantel's foot came down on something sharp. She gasped and fell back against the couch, lifting her leg. A small shard of glass stuck into the pad of her big toe. She pulled it out and looked at the floor. Shattered glass lay in a circular spray where someone—probably herself—had dropped it.

"Amelia?" she called, louder this time. Still nothing. Chantel skirted the broken glass and searched the entire upstairs for her daughter, panic rising in her chest and shrilling her voice. The last place to look was the basement, but there was no way Amelia would be down there. Not alone. But it was the only place left and Amelia had to be there, because if she wasn't, Chantel would lose her *goddamn* mind.

Amelia is all I have, she thought, taking the stairs two at a time, ignoring the pain in her big toe. She called out to her daughter as she went, gripping the handrail, and dove into the darkness, hand outstretched for the pull cord. She snagged it, nearly falling as the light bulb burst to life and swung wildly by its cord. The laundry room door was closed. She liked to keep it open, otherwise it got too cold in there. She opened the door.

Amelia huddled in a ball, face against her folded arms and bent knees. The smallest little ball of a child.

"Amelia," Chantel breathed her daughter's name. Amelia lifted her red, tear-stained face. Her little features crumpled. Chantel reached for her and she shied away. Chantel dropped to one knee and opened her arms. Amelia gave in and ran into them, sobbing against her mother's neck. Thick, wet sobs.

"What are you doing in here, sweetheart?"

Amelia bawled her answer, but Chantel couldn't understand her. She stroked her daughter's back and shushed her gently. When Amelia's sobs turned into soft hiccups, Chantel asked again.

"What were you doing in there?"

A fat tear rolled down Amelia's cheek. "Mama," she said, sniffling and hiccuping. "You put me in there."

Chantel's mind swarmed, looking for a memory of putting her child—her only child who she knew was afraid of the basement—in the very area she feared the most. But nothing surfaced.

The wine.

Chantel carried little Amelia up the stairs and tucked her into the big master bed before going back down to clean up the mess in the living room. Broken glass. Empty bottles. A spill of something that turned out to be urine. She gagged.

Who made this mess? She felt like someone had knocked her out, locked her daughter in the basement, and had a party.

Chantel went back down the stairs to the laundry room. She stood in the doorway and looked around, wondering why she would have put her daughter in this room.

Down by the floor beside the washing machine was a large hole in the wall. Chantel crouched down and peered inside. It was dark in there. Though they didn't have any issues with vermin, she wondered if other animals could be living in there.

On the shelf where she laid clothes that had to "lay flat to dry" sat a flashlight. She snatched it and clicked it on.

The light was dim, but it reached into the darkness enough to see it was more than a hole. It was a short tunnel about ten or twelve feet deep. There was nothing in there. No flash of feral eyes. No scat. Not even a whiff of animal waste.

She couldn't spot any animal tracks in the loose dirt and gravel floor within the tunnel, either. She clicked off the light and sat where she had found Amelia, as far from that hole as she could get. It made sense why her daughter would fear this room. If she was honest with herself, that hole was creepy and needed to be patched up.

When Chantel finished investigating, she went back to Amelia's side.

"My sweet girl," she said, stroking Amelia's hair. "What happened?"

Amelia pulled the blankets up to her chin and looked at Chantel with big, watery eyes. She gave the faintest of head shakes. Chantel pulled the blanket down.

"You told me not to say anything," Amelia whispered. "You told me it was a game."

"What was a game?"

Amelia's brows creased upward. Her lower lip trembled. "You woke me up. You said your name was Melba, and I was a naughty girl, and I should run from you." Her voice hitched. Her little chest heaved. Chantel pulled Amelia into her arms and kept stroking her hair and back.

She didn't remember this game, but she knew Amelia was telling the truth. Amelia was so frightened of the laundry room, there was no way she would hide there all night just to make up this outrageous story.

"What did you do?" Chantel asked quietly. She realized then her pulse pounded.

"I ran." Amelia's voice squeaked. "But you caught me and you took me down there. You said I had to face the monster. Strong girls face their fears, you said." Her little voice was barely audible.

Chantel hugged her daughter tight. A tear fell from her eye. She couldn't fathom doing this to her baby girl. Her life, her love, her soul. Her everything.

"I think you left," Amelia whispered after a few moments of quiet sobbing. "I think you left the house. You left me in the laundry room and locked the door and you left." Her breathing came faster. Her little face cracked, and she bawled again.

Chantel rocked Amelia until her quiet sobs silenced and she became heavy in Chantel's arms. She lay Amelia down against the pillows.

You said your name was Melba.

Melba? Like the toast? she wondered as she closed the door to a crack. She stood in the hallway and took a deep breath.

That all happened on Wednesday.

On Saturday, rain pounded against the windows, and wind whipped the trees. Chantel pulled out some paper and crayons and they sat at the dining room table. Not at the far ends from each other like they did when they played Royals, but together. Amelia was at the head and Chantel to her right. They both had paper. Amelia dumped the whole box of crayons on the table, not a care for keeping them organized by color or sharpness or anything like that. She liked to see them all in plain sight. Having to pull them out by their tips was inefficient, she once told Chantel. Chantel wasn't sure where her daughter had learned the word *inefficient*, but she must have picked it up from school or something.

Chantel drew a face. She loved to draw eyes and full lips.

"Amelia," Chantel said. "Tell me why you're so afraid of the laundry room."

Amelia's tongue stuck out the side of her mouth as she scribbled a gray crayon and made a cloud in the sky of her artwork.

"Because you told me there is a monster in there," Amelia said. "You told me the monster would come and get me if I didn't behave." She looked up at Chantel and cocked her head. "Remember?" She looked down at her paper and kept drawing. "You said it would snack on my bones and flesh."

Chantel plucked at her lower lip. Something she'd started doing lately when she was concerned or worried or confused. She peeled a small scrap of skin from her lower lip, wincing when it peeled a touch too far. She sucked her lip into her mouth, tasted blood.

"The monster lives in the hole in the wall by the

washing machine," Amelia said. She kept drawing, now the blue crayon shaded in the sky with a puffy cloud.

Chantel picked up a pink crayon and fiddled with it. "Have we played any other games lately? Different from the fairies and royal people games?"

Amelia shook her head. "Just that one time when you were Melba. But Melba hasn't come back ever since."

Chantel tucked her lips into her mouth and took a deep breath through her nose.

"You're sure Melba was me? She wasn't someone else?"

Amelia kept shading in the sky. She gave a one-shoulder shrug. "I don't know."

Chantel knew *I don't know* meant Amelia didn't understand the question. She often used not knowing as an escape to avoid saying, "I don't get what you mean." Maybe to avoid feeling foolish.

"Did Melba look exactly like me?" Chantel didn't even know why she was asking this, other than maybe it was some impostor who'd knocked her out and taken over for a while. She hadn't even thought to check if the jewels were still in the jewelry boxes upstairs.

I didn't think to check, because they aren't mine.

Amelia pursed her lips to the side and looked up at the corner. "Well, sort of. But your face was different."

"Different how?" Chantel asked. Eye color would be the most obvious. A mustache maybe—

"It looked more—" Amelia shook her head. "I don't know."

"More what?" Chantel was desperate for an answer.

Amelia stopped coloring. She took a deep breath and met Chantel's eyes.

"She looked like you—I mean you as Melba looked like you—but her face was...evil."

Evil. Chantel didn't know her daughter knew that word.

"I didn't like that game, Mama. I don't want Melba to come back, okay?"

Chantel nodded, but she didn't say a word, afraid her voice would break.

"She's the one who told me about the monster," Amelia whispered. Chantel wasn't sure she'd heard correctly. "I thought it was you, but I'm pretty sure it was her." Her voice quavered. "You wouldn't tell me anything like that...would you?"

Chantel shook her head. "Never, baby. Never ever. I'd never do anything to hurt you."

The next day, Chantel located a highly rated child therapist and made an appointment. The doctor—Sheila Montgomery—had an opening later that afternoon, so Chantel took it, anxious to get Amelia in. They sat together in the room and talked about what had brought them in that day. After the introductions and pleasantries and Chantel telling the therapist about Melba—leaving out the part in which she blacked out and woke to find empty wine bottles strewn about—Dr. Montgomery asked Chantel if she could speak with Amelia alone.

"Is that...typical?" Chantel asked. She felt okay leaving the two of them alone together, since Sheila was a woman, but she thought Amelia had told her everything. A sudden icy fear slid into her veins. What if Amelia *hadn't* told her everything about Melba?

"I assure you," Sheila said. "This is customary."

Chantel nodded and slid her purse onto her shoulder. "I'll just be right out here, Amelia." She turned and went to the door. "Everything'll be okay, okay? You can trust the doctor."

Amelia nodded.

Chantel sat in the waiting room and picked up a magazine, flipping through it while straining to listen. When she couldn't hear a thing, she got up and pressed her ear to the door, but the therapist had a sound machine running on the inside of the door that drowned out anything going on inside.

She didn't like this. Not one bit. She should have fought back. She should have—

The door opened. Chantel leaped back, gripping her purse strap with both hands.

Sheila ushered Amelia out, without touching her, Chantel noted. "Go play with the puzzle toys over there in the corner, Amelia. I just need to talk to your mom for a second, okay?"

Amelia made a beeline for the toys. Wooden beads on a thick wire that she ran up and around and down and under and loopty-looping.

"It's like a roller coaster, Mama." Amelia smiled and ran the train of beads around again.

Sheila motioned for Chantel to come back inside the office. She didn't close the door all the way. They could hear the beads clacking on the roller coaster toy as Amelia ran them back and forth on the wire track.

"What did she say?" Chantel asked.

"She talked about someone named Melba," Sheila said. "Is this someone living in your home?"

Chantel closed her eyes and bit her lips. She took a deep breath. "Melba is someone I apparently pretended to be one night."

"Multiple times, actually."

Light flashed at the edges of Chantel's eyes. "Multiple —but—"

Sheila held her hands up. "It's what she told me. Do you remember these games? Amelia mentioned she enjoyed playing make believe, but not when Melba was around."

Chantel was taken aback. Multiple times... Amelia hadn't let on that Melba had been around more than twice. Once to tell her the story about the monster and once the other night when she locked her in the laundry—

"What did she tell you about Melba?" Chantel asked.

"Melba frightens her. With good reason. If she's someone living with you, I would encourage you to speak with her about her interactions with your daughter. They are harmful and, frankly, abusive."

Heat prickled Chantel's eyes. Her vision blurred. A tear dripped onto her cheek.

"There is no one else living with us," she confessed. "I think... I think *I'm*...Melba."

Sheila's mouth tightened, but her eyes softened. "I have someone I think you should speak with. A psychiatrist."

"Can't I speak with you?"

Sheila shook her head while she opened a desk drawer and pulled out a card. "I'm afraid I specialize in child and adolescent therapy only. But Dr. Shore can help. He specializes in mental disorders."

"Mental disorders?" Chantel touched her throat. "Do you think—?"

Sheila held her hands up in surrender. "Call Dr. Shore. He'll be able to help you."

Chantel took the card and tucked it into her purse.

"Shall we make an appointment for next week? For Amelia?"

At home, Chantel held the cordless phone in one hand, Dr. Shore's card in the other. She'd dialed and canceled the call three times already.

He specializes in mental disorders.

Mental disorders? What could she possibly have?

She dialed again and held the phone to her ear. This time, she followed through and made an appointment for the next day while Amelia would be at school. After she hung up, she plucked at her lip.

"Mama?" Amelia stood in the doorway, big eyes wide and uncertain. Chantel held her arms open.

"Come here, my girl," she said. Amelia went to her. Chantel pulled Amelia onto her lap and wrapped her in her arms.

"I'm sorry if you got in trouble at that lady's office today," Amelia said.

"I didn't get in trouble. Don't worry." She hugged her baby girl close, breathed in her little girl scent. "Shall we put on some jewels and have a lovely dinner in the formal dining room tonight?" Chantel changed her voice to sound like royalty.

Amelia giggled. "Yes!"

Chantel started dinner while Amelia ran upstairs to

pick her jewels. Chantel always gave her first pick, and Amelia always came down with a diamond-encrusted tiara, strings of pearls, diamonds, rubies. Her fingers were too little to wear the rings, and she didn't have pierced ears, so she left the rings and earrings for Chantel. Aside from the jewels left behind by the previous owners, there was also a fur wrap and a variety of elbow-length gloves, which Amelia always put on as well. The gloves were so long they went up to her armpits, and she always picked the white ones.

She came downstairs dressed as expected.

"When shall I expect to dine this eve?" she asked.

"In just a moment, mum. Dinner's almost ready," Chantel said in a cockney accent.

"I'll be in the parlor. Fetch me when it's time." Amelia turned on her heel and left, walking like she was on stage in a pageant.

Chantel laughed quietly while she finished up their dinner. Nothing special. Some leftover chicken and pasta. She dished plates and tented them in foil before running upstairs to get her jewels on.

She sat at the vanity and put on earrings, rings, bracelets, and a few necklaces. She looked up and met her eyes in the mirror.

"Take those off," her reflection said. "They don't belong to you."

Chantel jumped up and backed away from the mirror, but her reflection still sat at the vanity on the other side of the glass.

"Take them off! They aren't yours!" The woman in the mirror looked just like her, but...evil.

"Melba?" Chantel whispered.

The reflection dipped its chin and grinned in such a malicious way, Chantel felt her blood turn to ice. This was the creature who had abused her daughter.

"You," she rushed the mirror. "You leave my daughter alone. Do you hear me? You can harass me all you want, but you leave my Amelia alone!"

"Mama?"

Chantel whirled. Amelia stood in the doorway.

"Are you okay, Mama?"

Chantel looked back in the mirror. She lifted her hand. Her reflection matched the movement. The face was hers. Not an evil visage. But there, just behind her, something moved with her, but just a fraction of a second off. Melba was there. Hiding.

"Oh my," Chantel said, touching her pearls. "You startled me. I'm just fine. Having a discussion with my reflection. When you're old and wrinkled like me, you must give yourself pep talks."

"You're not old and wrinkled. You're lovely."

Chantel forced a smile and ushered Amelia back downstairs.

They ate their dinner and afterward, Amelia went up to take off her jewels and get ready for bed while Chantel cleaned up. As she scraped the remains of noodles and cream sauce into the trash, she wondered if Melba was the name of the previous owner. She wondered if the house was haunted by that woman's malignant spirit.

Given the circumstances of the previous owners' death, it made sense they might come back to haunt the place. Or to haunt *her* specifically.

Chantel had followed them. She wanted to ask them about their house. Ask them if they'd ever thought about selling it. They were old. Certainly, the two of them didn't need all that space to maintain. The upkeep alone would probably end up killing them.

They were in their old Ford car on the road to town. Chantel thought maybe they were going out for breakfast and assumed they would pull into the local greasy spoon, but they drove on past it and kept going through town and onto the curving road that wound through the woods.

Though she didn't remember every detail of the incident, Chantel remembered the sun dappling the road, sometimes glinting off the chrome bumper of their old car, momentarily blinding her.

She wove around a tight corner, and her purse toppled over, dumping the contents onto the floorboard.

"Shit," Chantel whispered. She reached for it.

They had slowed to take the next corner. Chantel's head was below dash level, hand reaching. She sat up just in time to brake, but it wasn't enough.

It was just a kiss, her bumper against theirs, just the right—or wrong—angle to spin them out of control, off the road, and down into a ravine.

Chantel slammed on the brakes, eyes wide, heart pounding. She pulled over, hands gripping the wheel. They shook when she reached for the door handle. She got out on shaky legs, groped along the side of her car, and peered over the edge.

Their car lay upside down. The front left tire spun in a wobbly circle, dangling from a broken axle.

It was a long way down, almost vertical. No one cried for help. No one cried at all.

"Hello?" Chantel called, but her voice only barely cracked through. She stepped down onto the path the tires had made and picked her way down, crying out every time she slipped, sure she would break her leg or her neck.

When she reached the car, she crouched next to the driver's side window and peered in.

The old couple dangled from their seatbelts. Blood dripped from the wife's forehead. Chantel reached through the broken window and felt the husband's neck for a pulse.

He was dead.

She moved around the car to the passenger side. Blood pooled on the ceiling of the overturned car. So much blood. The smell of it strong and metallic. Chantel reached in. The woman's eyes opened and met Chantel's. She jerked her hand back.

"Help." The woman's lips formed the word. Her face crumpled into sadness and fear.

"I'm so sorry," Chantel said. "I'll get help."

The woman sucked in a ragged gasp of air, eyes still on Chantel.

"I'll be right back." Chantel stood and looked up the hill at how far their car had tumbled.

The next thing she remembered was standing at the top of the hill, staring down at where the car lay. Dirt and cuts covered her hands. Her clothes were destroyed. Something gouged her left palm. Her fist was closed around something. She opened her hand.

A house key.

Chantel's purse was still on the floorboard, its contents

spilled everywhere. She drove back into town, but never called for help.

She and Amelia moved into the house a week later.

Sheila Montgomery had sent information ahead, so when Chantel met Dr. Shore, he already knew about Melba.

"Tell me about her," he said in a calm and pleasant voice. Chantel sat on the edge of a couch across from him, unable to relax.

"I don't know anything about her," Chantel said. "Only what Amelia told me."

He nodded. "Sheila sent me some notes." He consulted them.

They talked about Chantel's history. Did she have any trauma as a child or young adult? No. Did she have any trauma as an adult, abusive relationships, things like that? Chantel gulped and said no.

She knew she should have been honest about the car crash, but she didn't want to go to prison for killing an innocent couple. Accident or not, she didn't call an ambulance, and she didn't call the police, and no one else reported it either.

"Have you ever experienced lost time? Like you come to or wake up and time has passed with no recollection of what happened?"

Chantel bit her lip. She nodded and told him about the chardonnay, which led to telling him about the figure in the mirror, telling her to take off the jewels. The jewels, she told him, were family heirlooms.

"I think our house is haunted," she whispered, plucking at her ragged lip.

Dr. Shore recommended Chantel keep a journal to document the incidents when she lost time, seeing the figure in the mirror, and anything that Amelia told her. He said to write about what happened prior to the events occurring and what happened after.

"We may be able to find some patterns. You could have some sort of trauma living within you that you just don't know about yet. Blacking out could be your brain's way of protecting you from remembering it."

Chantel nodded, though she knew exactly what the trauma was.

She kept a journal for several years, documenting and detailing the events of their lives. Melba didn't show up again until Amelia reached puberty and started acting out. Angry, sad, despondent, angry again. Chantel knew her daughter was grappling with hormones and new feelings and emotions, but she wasn't sure how to handle it all. She'd become Amelia's verbal punching bag.

One night, when Amelia was a week away from turning fifteen, during a shouting match in which Amelia aired all of her grievances, Chantel found out that Melba had made an appearance again. Many times, by the sound of it.

"Why do you even pretend? I know it's you. It's just your way of being a bitch without taking ownership of what you say or do." Tears streamed down Amelia's face. "You're *horrible*. I can't wait to turn eighteen so I can get the fuck out of here."

"Amelia!" Chantel had never heard her daughter curse before. But worse was the fact that she hadn't told Chantel about Melba coming back. They'd made an agreement years ago that Amelia would be honest and open and tell her whenever there was a Melba incident.

"I should get emancipated, like Kate."

"Kate's father *abused* her," Chantel cried.

"*You* abuse *me*, Mom." Amelia's words were acid. "It's *you*. Not *Melba*. And it's always after you've been drinking."

"Drinking? I don't drink!"

"If you don't believe me," Amelia said, disgusted, "check the recycling." She stormed up the stairs. Even though she was expecting it, she still winced when Amelia's door slammed.

The recycling? It was Amelia's job to take the trash and recycling out and to take the bins to the curb each week. Chantel went out to the garage and lifted the lid on the first recycle bin. On top was a collection of torn-up envelopes and junk mail. She shifted it to the side and underneath were multiple empty chardonnay bottles.

Chantel lifted a hand to her horrified face. She went back inside and stood at the bottom of the stairs. She wanted to apologize to Amelia. But she needed to know more. What was the extent of the damage Melba had caused?

She climbed the stairs and started with her journals. Amelia would need more time to cool off anyway. Chantel flipped through the numerous journals she'd written over the years, but nothing jumped out at her. No lost time. Nothing from Amelia. Not even a mention of Melba. She took the journals back to the bookcase and shoved them onto the shelf. Something fell onto the floor with a loud thud. Chantel jumped back with a short scream.

A hardbound journal with a leather cover lay on the floor. It looked like a book from an old library, but when Chantel opened it, she knew what it was.

Heavy-handed all-capital letters filled the pages.

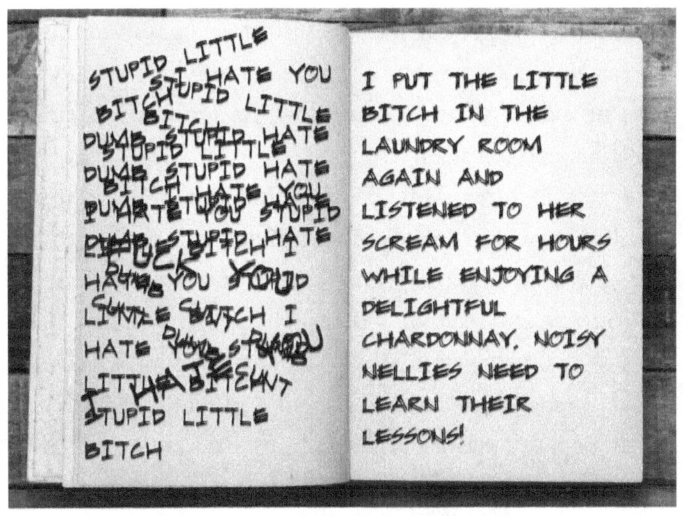

I PUT THE LITTLE BITCH IN THE LAUNDRY ROOM AGAIN AND LISTENED TO HER SCREAM FOR HOURS WHILE ENJOYING A DELIGHTFUL CHARDONNAY. NOISY NELLIES NEED TO LEARN THEIR LESSONS!

Chantel took Melba's journal to Dr. Shore. He prescribed her an anti-psychotic while tears dribbled down her face.

An anti-psychotic. How had it come to this? How had they not seen this before?

Because Amelia didn't tell me. Because I've been living a lie for almost a decade.

After finding Melba's journal, she had pulled the vanity bench over to the bookshelf and reached on top. There were three total. All documenting her anger at Amelia. Her treatment of Amelia. How scared Amelia was when she came around. How Amelia begged for *Mommy* to stop and to let Chantel back in. How she threatened Amelia's life if she told Chantel about her.

Chantel picked up her prescription and immediately dry swallowed a dose. She'd stopped crying long enough to drive up to the pharmacy window. As soon as she pulled away, the tears fell again.

I'm a monster. Was all she could think. She slapped herself. She needed to cross-check Melba's journals with her own. Put together a timeline. See if there was anything in *her* journal entries that would tell her *Melba* had been there. Any missing time. Any odd behavior from Amelia.

Had she chalked up Amelia's pulling away, their drifting apart, as *puberty*? Something that was supposed to happen between mother and daughter?

Amelia was still at school when Chantel got home. Melba's journals in her arms, she shuffled up the stairs sniffling. She turned into her bedroom and dropped the books.

Melba stood on top of the vanity bench, arms stretched up, hand patting the top of the bookshelf, searching for her journals.

As soon as they fell from Chantel's arms and hit the floor, Melba whirled around. She flickered as if a hologram. Chantel reached out for the doorframe, suddenly dizzy. She fell against it, bounced off and hit the floor.

Melba's feet flickered toward her. She crouched and

grinned that evil grin. Melba *did* look just like her. Chantel was almost glad to see that she was a real person.

But then she flickered again and blinked out completely. Chantel closed her eyes.

She came to on the floor with Melba's journals around her.

Chantel looked at her watch. She wasn't sure what time she got home, but the timestamp on the prescription receipt told her not much time had passed, which meant she had *lost* no time. Which meant the drugs worked.

She was nervous and excited for Amelia to come home. Had an entire speech prepared about how sorry she was, how she found Melba's journals, but now she had medication that worked, and they could be happy again.

But she also had to confront Amelia.

Why hadn't Amelia told her about Melba? There was so much trauma there, it was no wonder her daughter hated her.

Chantel wanted to be open and honest with her daughter and wanted Amelia to be open and honest with her, so they could possibly mend the rift between them and get past all of it.

When Amelia came in, she froze in the doorway, hand on the door handle. Chantel was waiting in the grand entry with a plate of cookies.

Amelia slid her backpack off her shoulders and dropped it onto the floor.

"Uh, hi?" Amelia said. "What's going on?"

Chantel cleared her throat and instantly regretted the Suzy Homemaker act. It didn't feel right. It might have worked if Amelia was under ten, but she was sixteen now.

"I have some things I need to talk to you about." Chantel prepared to go into her speech, but her daughter's disdain froze the words in her mind. She opened and closed her mouth.

"Spit it out, Mom." Amelia crossed her arms. Her glower could have wilted the freshest of fresh flowers.

"Why didn't you tell me about Melba?" she blurted. "I found her journals." This was not how she wanted to start, but under Amelia's suspicious and hateful glare, her words failed her. She wanted to start with the drugs, how they worked to suppress Melba. "I got some drugs from Dr. Shore—"

"Good for you." Amelia grabbed her backpack and headed up the stairs. "I didn't tell you about Melba because you threatened to kill me. Okay? *You* threatened me, and stop acting like Melba is someone else. She's you. She's your, I don't know, excuse to be mean to me and treat me like shit." Amelia's face turned red and her lip trembled, but she didn't cry.

"Amelia, I'm sorry." Chantel took a step forward.

"Too little too late, Mom." Amelia stomped up the stairs.

She graduated a year later, and though Chantel was almost certain Melba hadn't shown up since she started taking her medication every night, their relationship was never the same.

In the morning, after they'd had a glass of real champagne together and reminisced about when they first moved in, Amelia was gone. Left like a thief in the night. Chantel called her, but she didn't answer.

"Please, just tell me you're okay," Chantel pleaded on her daughter's voicemail.

She got a text back. *I'm fine. Stop calling me.*

Chantel held her phone to her chest. Relief and sadness crumpled her face.

She tried for several years to keep in touch with Amelia, but Amelia made it clear she wanted nothing to do with her mother.

Chantel wondered if it hurt Amelia as much as it hurt her, but no. It was Melba's fault. Melba did this to them. Forced this wedge between them.

She closed the door to Amelia's room and never looked in it again, but closing the door did not close her mind to the onslaught of guilt that came from Amelia's secret departure. Chantel knew her daughter was gone from her life forever. No amount of begging and pleading would bring her back.

A few years into her lonely and solo life, there was a knock on the door. Chantel had taken to staying in bed late. She didn't go to the door. She peered out the window. A police cruiser was parked out front.

Chantel put a hand to her mouth. Was it Amelia? Had something happened to her? A neighbor—Stan—out walking his dog stopped and called to them. Two officers came into view off the front porch. They spoke on the sidewalk, occasionally throwing glances and hand gestures at the house. After a minute or two, the cops climbed back into their car. Stan waited for them to leave, waving them away, before jogging up to the front porch.

The doorbell rang.

Chantel pulled on her robe and hurried down the stairs. She flung the door open.

"Chantel," Stan said, eyeing her appearance. She likely looked ghastly. "The police were here, did you hear them?"

She shook her head. "I haven't been feeling well. Feverish sleep. I thought I might have heard something, but I've just been so tired," she said in a breathy voice.

"Well, I got rid of them for you." He grinned. Chantel thought he had liked her off and on. Maybe he was just neighborly. She never gave him a second thought, because she always had Amelia to care for.

Chantel pulled her robe closer around her, clenching it at her throat. "What did they want?" she asked.

He smiled and patted his dog, sitting politely at his heel. "They, um, it sounds like they maybe found the old folks who used to live here."

Chantel's heart stopped. Almost literally. She coughed and choked and pounded her own chest. She had counted her blessings every year that went by without news of the couple being found, and after a time, she thought she could forget the whole thing.

"Ah, that's a nasty cough." The neighbor backed away and tugged at the leash. "Don't worry," he called as he backed away. "I won't tell anyone."

Chantel looked up as he gave her an exaggerated wink.

"See you around."

She hurried inside and closed the door behind her, leaning back.

"You knew this would come some day, didn't you?" Melba's voice said from the mirror over the decorative table.

Chantel closed her eyes and took deep breaths while waves of nausea washed over her. She doubled over, retching and sobbing at the same time. Horrible sounds ripped from her throat.

After that, she started losing time again. Large chunks of time. Melba's journals filled with stories of *fucking* Stan. She covered her mouth as she read the jagged handwriting. The graphic detail of her sexual trysts with him. She bawled and threw the journal across the room. Then she retrieved it and ripped it apart, screaming with each chunk of pages she destroyed. She pulled the others down from their hiding spot on top of the bookcase and did the same until every page had been destroyed and her hands bled with paper cuts.

She held them in her lap and sobbed.

"I'm so sorry," she cried. Not to Melba. To the elderly couple she'd *killed*. To Amelia who she'd estranged. Who *Melba* had estranged. "You win," she whispered, snot running down her lip. She wiped at it furiously. "You win."

Chantel woke in the laundry room. Wet sounds came from the hole in the wall near the washing machine.

Amelia's monster. *Melba's* monster.

Chantel got to her hands and knees and gripped the edge of the drying shelf. Her legs shook when she tried to stand. Her vision swam. She closed her eyes and remembered.

She'd stopped taking her medication for a few days. Melba had come back gradually. First the figure in the mirror. Then speaking to Chantel in the mirror. Finally, she was there. She was out. Chantel had only ever seen Melba as a flickering hologram just before the medication suppressed her. But this Melba had substance. A physical presence.

"It's so good to be free," Melba had said, stretching.

Chantel had attacked first. She wanted to strangle this woman, this creature. They wrestled to the top of the stairs. Chantel twisted and flung Melba down. Gave a whoop at her triumph, but Melba grabbed her ankle at the last second and Chantel toppled down with her.

They landed on at the bottom in a heap, momentarily dazed. Chantel took stock. She was okay. Nothing hurt except her right shin. Melba groaned. Chantel leaped on top of her, hands wrapped around the evil woman's throat.

Melba struggled, still smiling her wicked smile. Still looking like Chantel, but different. Evil.

"You...can't...win," Melba said. With a surge of strength, she knocked Chantel off of her. Chantel fell to the side. Melba kicked her legs and caught Chantel in the face. Her nose crunched. Blood spilled. She grabbed her face, but Melba grabbed her upper arm and a fistful of Chantel's hair.

Melba dragged Chantel down the basement stairs, kicking and screaming. Near the bottom, Chantel got a little leverage with her legs dragging behind her on the stairs. She bundled them beneath her and shoved with all her might. Melba pitched forward, let go, and landed in a heap at the bottom in the darkness.

Chantel landed on her back, the wind knocked out of her. She took small gasps of air trying to get her breath back.

The light came on. Melba stood over her. She lifted her foot and brought it down on Chantel's face.

And now, here she was. Locked in the laundry room listening to something deep within that hole.

She said it would snack on my bones and flesh. Amelia's little voice.

Melba's monster was in there.

The crunch of dirt and gravel.

Melba's monster was coming.

When it emerged from the dark hole, it wore Melba's face but had fangs and sharp claws. It crawled out on its hands and knees and lunged at her. Chantel reflexively kicked her foot out and hit it square in the face, rocking its head back. It lunged again. Chantel rolled under it. It hit the door, cracking it. Shaking it in its frame. Affronted by the collision, the monster smashed the door. Clawed at it. It turned back to Chantel, leaped again. Chantel again rolled under it and ran out the door, up the stairs, and outside. She slammed doors behind her.

"Melba! Call your monster off!" Chantel shrieked.

Laughter came from behind her.

Melba.

Chantel whipped around. It was the monster. No, it was Melba. The claws slid back into her fingertips. The fangs shortened to normal teeth.

Chantel shook her head. They were the same thing.

Melba ran toward Chantel, teeth and claws re-emerging. Chantel sprinted for the front door and out into the night. Her instinct was to run, so she did.

The edge of the woods was a darker line in the darkness ahead.

An hour later, Melba emerged from the edge of the forest as dawn broke. Her claws retracted. She licked the blood from her fingers as her fangs shortened into normal teeth. She didn't kill Chantel but left her mangled in the woods. Face flayed open. The woman would suffer. Oh, she would suffer. The thought of it made Melba smile.

She entered the house. So quiet now. So peaceful. She climbed the stairs and put on the jewels like Chantel had. She gazed at herself in the mirror, her image strong and steady. No more flickering in and out of existence. No more waiting her turn. No more latching on to Chantel's guilt in order to emerge. She was here, and she was free.

She waltzed downstairs and cleaned up the mess Chantel had left. Straightened rugs, wiped up blood. In the basement, intent on fixing the door—or removing it altogether—a jagged pain struck her in the back. She stumbled forward toward the laundry room, catching herself on the edge of the doorframe.

She gasped for air and looked behind her, expecting Chantel, face flaps fluttering, to be there with some sort of blunt weapon. But there was no one there.

The pain hit her again. She clutched the necklaces draped around her neck. She held her ring-adorned hands up in front of her. They flickered. One ring dropped onto the floor, bounced and rolled away.

"No, no, no." She looked down at herself. "No!" The last one ripped from her vocal chords with the voice of the monster. The claws extended, retracted, extended. The beast wanted to flee the pain. Fear coursed through her veins. Primal thoughts battled with human thoughts. She fought the beast, reached toward the laundry room doorway, to leave to go back upstairs, but the beast's fear overtook her.

It dragged her into the hovel with her own hands, claws reaching and extending.

The jewels dropped from her as she lost substance. As her being faded into nonexistence.

She'd gone too far. Chantel must have died. Melba realized, far too late, their connection was more than mental. She couldn't survive without Chantel.

Her fear gave the monster the last ounce of strength it needed to take over completely.

The beast crawled as far back into the hole as it could go, fleeing the pain. It gave out a shuddering moan and curled into a ball. With a violent tremor, all breath released from its lungs.

The teeth went back to their human form.

The claws retracted one last time.

Melba exhaled one last breath.

Amelia's Monster Part 3: Secrets and Scars

IF ONLY WHAT WAS SAID COULD BE TAKEN BACK

Amelia stared down at the figure covered in a sheet on the table. She didn't know what she would find here, since the mummified corpse in her mother's basement had to have been her mother.

"You won't recognize her," the detective said. He reached for the sheet, but Amelia stopped him.

She lifted the side of the sheet where her mother's arm would be—if this was her mother—and looked for the tattoo.

The tattoo didn't have a good story behind it like some do. It didn't have any special meaning. Her mom had gotten it on her eighteenth birthday because she could. It was her way of marking her legal adulthood. It was a stylized butterfly on the inside of her wrist.

So original, Mom.

And there it was on the inside of the body's wrist.

This corpse was, in fact, her mother.

"It's her." Amelia said the words without emotion, but inside confusion reigned.

There had to be some mistake. If her mother was here, who was the mummy in the laundry room hovel?

Amelia finished up at the station and drove back home. She shook her head. Not home. To her *mother's* house. How easily one slips back into old thinking patterns. She parked out front and, inside the house, stood in the grand entry.

There had to be some explanation. She had to see the inside of that *creature's* wrist.

When she found the mummified corpse curled into the fetal position at the end of the tunnel, she didn't investigate it. She bonked her head on the joists above her, stifled a scream, and backed out as fast as she could. She'd crab crawled backward once she was in the laundry room proper and hit her back against the wall in the far corner.

A place she'd huddled so many times in her youth.

Amelia had called no one about the body. She also didn't mention it to the detectives. Her only reason was, she needed answers before involving anyone else. Gazing around the grand entry now, she took a deep, determined breath and made her way up the stairs. Her mother's room made the most sense as a starting place on the hunt for answers.

She hadn't been in her mother's room in a long time. Certainly not anytime after their relationship ripped apart. She'd kept her distance from her mom as much as possible.

Amelia gripped the doorknob, steeled herself, and pushed the door open.

Everything lay under a layer of dust.

At the vanity against the wall, where the things her mom used every day sat, Amelia lifted the hairbrush and shook the dust from it. She wiped her hand across the mirror and cleared away a circle of reflective surface, shocked at her pallid reflection. The fright in her eyes.

Amelia bit her lips. Something over her shoulder in the mirror caught her attention. She turned. On the floor, torn pieces of paper and book bindings lay in a pile. Amelia crouched next to them and lifted a few of the scraps.

Heavy jagged handwriting filled the fragments of paper. Dirty and foul words scribbled deep. It wasn't her mother's handwriting. Chantel Langland had a beautiful cursive hand.

Sometimes crazy is crazy.

The lower shelf of the bookcase held a collection of journals. Amelia pulled the first one out. Her mother's gorgeous handwriting filled the pages. The date was from so long ago, Amelia would have been six.

Dear, well, diary, I guess. Dr. Shore asked me to keep a journal. I haven't kept one in so long, I'm afraid I'm not sure what to even write. He wanted me to document everything, in case we could figure out any patterns that happen before I lose time.

Amelia pulled out the last journal. The date on the first entry was from that night Amelia came home and her mom was there, smiling.

"Too little, too late," Amelia whispered. She suddenly remembered that day so clearly. Her mom had been excited to tell her something and Amelia had shut her down. She remembered being so angry.

She scoffed at the memory. "With reason." Her mind flashed to the hole in the laundry room wall.

She read the entry, half disinterested, until she came upon a sentence that turned her blood cold.

If she'd only told me about the times Melba came around, I could have had more to tell Dr. Shore. I've been living a lie all this time.

Amelia hadn't thought of Melba since graduation after she successfully snuck out and left for good. She felt like she had held her breath all the way to the train station, only breathing again when she was on the train and chugging away from that horrible place.

This horrible place.

Melba. The hateful woman her mom pretended to be. Her excuse to treat Amelia like shit and pretend to not remember.

Amelia's decades old anger bubbled up. She threw the journal against the wall with a cry.

A piece of paper flew out of it and drifted to the floor. It glided across the dust, barely leaving a trace. It was probably another *stupid* journal entry. Some poor-me-excuses diatribe. Amelia stomped over to it and snatched it from the floor.

It was a letter.

To Amelia.

Dear Amelia,

I'm never going to send this. You made it clear you don't want to speak to me, and I understand now. But I have to get everything out. Everything I remember, anyway.

That day I found you in the laundry room. I woke in a daze. I didn't know what had happened. I know if you ever read this, you won't believe me. If you ever read this, you'll probably roll your eyes at your overly dramatic mother.

Amelia stopped herself in mid eye roll. She let out a soft laugh through her nose and bit her lip.

"Good one, Mom." She kept reading.

The thing is, Amelia, I stopped drinking when I was pregnant with you. I never touched the stuff ever again, so when I woke up and there were wine bottles all around... I knew something wasn't right. But I didn't want to admit there was something wrong with me.

It was guilt, Amelia. I felt so much guilt. I never told you the truth behind our coming to live in this house—

Here, droplets of water—probably tears—melted the ink into the paper. Some of the words were hard to read, but Amelia figured them out through context.

Her mother had killed the couple who had lived here before them.

It was an accident, I swear, but not calling for help was not. It was a conscious decision. One that haunts me to this day.

Amelia stopped reading for a second. Aunt Amelia and Uncle Henry never existed then. They were made up. A lie her mother told her to hide her own guilt.

She groaned and couldn't tell if it was disgust or some sort of locked away torment finally breaking through. Probably both. She dropped the letter and wiped her hands on her pants. She suddenly felt sick. In the master bathroom she splashed water on her face, cupped her palm under the flowing water and drank as if she hadn't had water in days. She spat into the sink, and when the nausea passed, she dried her hands and face.

Her mother, the killer. Amelia was surprised she didn't blame the accident on *Melba*.

Amelia picked up the letter and read the rest.

I kept journals with the hope of finding...something. Patterns is what Dr. Shore said. But I found Melba's journals filled with hate for you. I didn't know Melba harmed you so much until then. And not until you told me.

By then, it was too little, too late. That's what you said to me. Too little, too late, Mom. I'll never forget those words. They play in my mind randomly, like the first notes of a song playing over and over. I wake up with them chanting in my head.

I didn't know phrases could get stuck in a person's head.

Amelia closed her eyes. She'd just thought that same thing that very morning.

Teeth...and claws. We found your mother. Teeth...and claws—

Only...it wasn't her mother. The realization struck her with a cold electric prickle that ran over her scalp and down her back. She shuddered and broke out in goosebumps.

"Oh, God."

The figure in the laundry room hovel. Not her mom. No. But that would mean... "Oh my God." Amelia stood and backed away from the journals. The letter fell from her hand.

If Chantel Langland lay dead in the morgue, that could only mean the curled and dried up figure in the basement could only be—

"Melba."

Amelia turned to the doorway. She had to see. To make sure she hadn't imagined it. It had been a stressful day, and now this? Regret fell on her shoulders like a physical weight. She dropped back onto the floor, onto her knees.

It had been someone else all along and she'd blamed her mother for lying to her. For pretending to be that vile woman. All the memories of Melba's torment, her abuse, came rushing back. Amelia gagged. She bent forward and dry heaved.

"I have to get out of here," she moaned. She crawled to the edge of her mother's bed and clawed herself to standing.

When she had her balance, she strode toward the door but stopped just after passing the vanity.

Something had caught her eye. Something strange. For a second, she thought she saw her reflection standing there, perfectly still, even while she stormed across the reflective surface.

She stepped backward. Her reflection followed. She crept closer to the mirror. Behind her, another figure crept closer, a fraction of a second after her.

Amelia whirled around. There was no one there.

When she turned back, her reflection grinned at her with her own face, but...evil.

Two hands shot out of the mirror and gripped her throat.

Family Plot

KEEPER OF A FAMILY TRADITION

"There was a girl," Mama said. "She tended a garden of stones. A man walked by every day and noticed her toiling away at the dirt, but nothing ever grew." Mama tucked the blankets around me and brushed a strand of hair off my forehead. "One day, he finally asked her, 'Little girl, what are you doing?'" Mama stroked my forehead, and as I drifted off to sleep, she finished the story. "Sir, the little girl said. I'm taking care of my family."

Every once in a while, Mama's voice still tells me this story in the space between sleep and full wakefulness. I wake up with tears on my cheeks. It was one of the last things she told me, and I often remember it when I feel like I have no one.

Mama died when I was five. Over the course of a year, if I remember right—time is different when you're little—she wasted away. A hard life will do that. In our last year together, I knew things were tough. She fought hard to keep me safe and secure. She worked hard. I remember she was gone a lot, and I had to learn to be on my own. I usually just cuddled into blankets on a couch that creaked whenever I moved. I had a teddy bear. I would sing to it and hold it close and wait for her to come home.

I'm sure it was drugs that took her from me, but she never used in front of me, so I can't be one hundred percent sure. There was one more thing she told me in our short time together.

"Family is the only thing in this world that is certain."

It might be true, but I didn't *have* any family now. Not since she died fifteen years ago. Any time her saying about family popped into my head, I scoffed and wondered where is my family? Where is my certainty?

I used to wish for comfort and safety, for a roof over my head. A hot meal. Any food really. Someone to—not love me—but to care for me. To be cared for.

Though, love would be nice, too, if I'm honest. But what is love, when you sell the illusion of it almost every night of the week?

Who hasn't wished for something better?

Even when a person is well off with a great job, benefits, a solid and regular salary, they still wish to win the lottery. They long for something better, different, more fulfilling. But when you have nothing, the lives those people hate are what you'd long to have.

I wanted out of this life. I wished for some weird and obscure relative to die off and bestow upon me all the riches they'd acquired over their lifetime. A mansion. More money than I'd ever spend in my lifetime.

Comfort.

Safety.

After the incident with Bruno—we *definitely* don't talk

about Bruno—I prayed for anything to take me out of this life.

He'd left me for dead when I used a small portion of my earnings for a snack. Just a candy bar! He took the rest with his fists and more.

I lay on the ground, bleeding, clothes torn. It started to rain. Naturally. Because rock bottom always comes with a side of shitty weather.

I rolled onto my back in the dark alley and let the rain soothe my beaten skin. Wash away the tears and the blood.

How did I get here? How could I get out? These are the questions I asked but already knew the answers to. But for some reason, you still ask them when you're in this situation. You always wonder how your life got the way it did, and if you trace it back—which you try not to do—you realize it was your own stupid and ignorant choices that got you there. Naïveté. The youthful hopes that come with aging out of foster care.

Rain drops pelted me. I closed my eyes and wished for... not someone to save me. No, I didn't want a savior—Bruno pretended to be my savior and look where that got me. I wanted a way out.

Preferably one in which I still lived. Trust me. Suicide had crossed my mind a time or two, but I didn't have the courage to take my own life. The afterlife was too, well, unknown.

I dragged myself to my feet, tested my balance carefully, hand outstretched toward the wall for support in case I fell. My head swam from the beating. I'm sure he gave me a concussion.

I took stock. I was okay. Bruised, sure, ego depleted, of course. I was also angry. At myself.

I mistook kindness for caring and put my faith in the wrong people. Someone told me you could choose your family, and I loved that, since I didn't have one. But I chose the wrong members to be my family.

And family *wasn't* certain like Mama said. When there's no one left, there's no certainty.

I pulled the shredded remains of my shirt around me and limped to the police station.

In this world, you walk into any establishment looking the way I did, and you get judged. Your pimp raping you is not a crime. It's something you had coming.

All I really wanted was to spend the night in a dry, clean enough place. I put on a good show stumbling around, slurring my words, and they threw me in the drunk tank. It wasn't my first time, though usually I was actually drunk when they did it.

I sank against the wall and took a deep breath.

***

In the morning, they let me out of the cell and I limped out into the daylight, dragging my shadow behind me like the ghost of my past and what could have been.

At the bottom of the steps a man in a bowler hat stood looking up at me. A bowler hat, in this era? Really? He pulled it off, though. Somehow. Probably the accompanying three-piece suit in the middle of summer. A gold chain draped from the pocket of his vest. He pulled at it and consulted a pocket watch.

I snorted. A pocket watch? I checked the cars in the immediate area to see if I'd maybe been transported back in time. Everything seemed normal.

"Miss Everett?" the man asked as I approached.

I tugged at my torn clothes. "Yeah?"

He didn't look me up and down like a possible john might. He held out his hand. I took it. He gave it a squeeze and a shake.

"I'm Mr. Davenport, executor of your Aunt Harriet's estate."

"I have an Aunt Harriet?"

He consulted an envelope in his hands. "You *are* Monica Everett, yes?"

"Yes," I said.

"I have instructions here to take you immediately to Dr. Harriet's home in the mountains." He motioned to a black town car at the curb. A driver got out and opened the back door.

"You'll find a change of clothes inside. I'll give you a few minutes to—eh—freshen up."

Mama had taught me not to get into a car with a stranger or to even talk to strangers, and definitely don't open the door to them, but when you hit rock bottom and someone shows up talking about estates, you get in the car. You have nothing to lose anyway.

The car windows were tinted so dark it felt like night inside the car. The clothes were a size too big and probably would have fit me about a year or two ago, but I wasn't going to complain. They were clean and intact.

When Mr. Davenport opened the door the dome light

nearly blinded me. He climbed in and sat across from me, facing me.

"Where is this estate?" I asked as the driver pulled away from the curb.

"In the mountains. Not too far." He smiled. It wasn't kind, but it also was not lewd or lecherous like I was used to. It was a courtesy smile, I realized. This guy was just doing his job.

I smiled back, but inside I wondered if I was being kidnapped. If I'd end up trafficked or killed. A statistic no one really cared about. No one would know I was missing except maybe Bruno. Probably not even Bruno.

We arrived about half an hour later, but I'm not sure because I fell asleep in the luxurious leather seat. I tried not to, but the lull of the smooth car ride took it right out of me. Plus, sleeping in a jail cell isn't exactly the Ritz-Carlton no matter how warm and dry it is compared to the street.

I woke when the car bumped and jostled off the pavement onto a dirt road.

"We've almost arrived," Davenport said.

We appeared to be traveling through a tunnel of trees. They opened up onto an expansive property with a fountain centered in a circular drive.

The house was something out of a Shirley Jackson novel. What? Just because I live on the street doesn't mean I don't read. The book was my mom's. She'd dog-eared pages and underlined passages and it was the closest thing I had to having her in my life.

"Wow," I whispered.

"Indeed," Mr. Davenport said, unimpressed. He probably saw estates like this all the time in his line of work.

The car came to a stop. I reached for the door handle but it was locked.

"Carl will get the door, Ms. Everett, but before you get out I must tell you a few things."

I sat back against the seat.

"You will be at the house for a few days with Dr. Harriet's staff."

"What happens after a few days?"

"I'll return for the reading of the will."

"You can't read the will now?"

He smiled again, and I couldn't tell if it was condescending or not. It felt like an aren't-you-precious kind of smile. It was that same courtesy smile he'd given me before.

"This is all in accordance with Dr. Harriet's wishes. I can tell you, however, the entire estate was left to you as her only living relative."

At this news, chills shivered over my arms. "What does the entire estate include?"

He chuckled. "That's for you to find out in a few days. I'll be back on Thursday. Enjoy the estate, Ms. Everett. I trust you'll not find it lacking for anything."

At that, Carl opened the door and Mr. Davenport dismissed me with a nod to the outside world.

The house towered above me. The window on the car rolled down.

"Oh, Ms. Everett, one more thing," Davenport said. "Don't leave the property until I come back to talk to you, or all will be forfeit."

It seemed odd, but given the fact I had nowhere else to go and wanted to avoid Bruno anyway, I had no desire to go back into the city any time soon. If this place had a bed and a stocked fridge, I wouldn't leave. Based on what Davenport said about Dr. Harriet's staff, I'd be well cared for.

I nodded. Davenport nodded back and rolled the window up. The car pulled away, circled around the fountain, and disappeared into the tunnel of trees flanking the driveway.

I looked up at the house. The mansion, I should say. The front door opened and a woman bustled out. She had a matronly appearance with wide hips and large bosom, graying hair pulled back in a bun. Her eyes were kind, as was her smile.

"You must be Monica," she said, coming down the steps. I met her halfway. "I'm Beverly, the housekeeper." She pulled me into a familiar embrace. For the brief moment before she released me, I melted into her. She let go and led me inside. "My husband keeps the grounds. You'll meet him at supper. We are here to ensure your stay is comfortable and you have everything you need. You'll meet the cook at noon when lunch is served."

I looked around the grand entry. A massive staircase climbed up to the second floor from the center. Hallways led down each side and doors led off into rooms to the left and right.

"You have your pick of any bedroom. May I recommend my favorites?"

I nodded. As we ascended the stairs to the second floor, Beverly pointed out some of the features of the house and told me about the rooftop balcony where I could see the entire property. She didn't stop talking the entire time.

"You're a quiet one, aren't you?" She beamed at me.

"I'm just...in shock, I think?"

She touched my arm. She had the face and demeanor of someone you felt like you could tell anything to. Someone you could trust.

"Mr. Davenport picked me up at the police station this morning."

Her features shifted to concern. Her grip on my arm tightened.

"I haven't lived the life of luxury my aunt did. That's all I'll say." I looked at the worn hardwood floor.

"Well, no one is perfect and someone must be shining down on you now to bring you here to us."

We completed the tour of the second floor. Of the seven options, I chose Beverly's favorite bedroom. It looked out on the lake behind the house. I didn't have any belongings with me, or in general, but Beverly told me she would have the boutique come. I told her what sizes I usually wore but she insisted on taking measurements.

"So thin," she said in a low voice with the tape measure around my waist.

I couldn't remember the last actual meal I'd had, other than the half candy bar I'd eaten before Bruno slapped it out of my hand.

My stomach growled as she let go of the tape measure around my waist.

A bell rang. "That's the lunch bell. Just in time, it sounds like." Beverly grinned.

A few days came and went. I lived the life of luxury I'd dreamed of my entire life. The life I'd wished for on the ground in the alley. I had never met and therefore had no idea who Dr. Harriet was, nor how I was connected to her, but I was afraid to ask. I didn't want the bubble to burst. What if I was the wrong Monica Everett?

Mr. Davenport arrived on Thursday like he said. He read the entire will at a big desk in the study—one of my favorite places in the house aside from the library. As he listed out everything included in the estate, I had to clench my teeth to keep my jaw from dropping.

My wish had been answered. I would never be without ever again. There was enough money for three lifetimes.

Mr. Davenport reached the end of the list and cleared his throat.

"Now, the terms." The way he said it dropped an ice bucket over my head. "The terms are the requirements to ensure you get to keep all of this." He waved around vaguely.

I hadn't thought about requirements or that I'd have to do something to keep this. It had only been a few days, but as I sat in a plush leather chair in designer clothes that fit perfectly and made me look like a lady, I'd grown used to the lifestyle already. I couldn't imagine going back to the loud city or Bruno or the life I had.

"Go on," I said, lifting my chin.

"There is only one condition," Davenport said.

"Okay," I said. "What is it? I'll do anything to stay here." I meant it.

Mr. Davenport slid a letter across the table. It had my name on the envelope.

"I'll leave you to read this. I received a copy as well. If you have any questions…well… I'm not sure I can answer them, but I can try." He stood and left me with the letter.

I tore it open. Aunt Harriet's handwriting was old school script and she wrote like she was from another time.

Dear Monica,

I know right now you probably have many questions about who I am and why you're here. You will learn all of this over time as you explore your new home and the grounds.

I trust you have enjoyed your stay thus far at the estate. Davenport has been watching you and told me all about your circumstances.

It delights me to offer you a new life.

This life does not come free, I'm afraid. While there is only one condition, it is a condition that will test your moral fiber and make you question if this is all worth it. It certainly did not appeal to your mother.

"My mother?" I whispered, but no one heard me because I was alone. I returned my attention to the letter.

In order to keep everything—the mansion, the grounds, the money—you only need to do one thing. It is imperative.

You must feed the garden.

I paused. Feed the garden? Like fertilize it? I'd walked most of the grounds and saw only one garden, overgrown with weeds and dying plants. Was I too late? I looked at the letter and kept reading.

The vultures will show you where it is.

The letter ended there. Vultures? Feed? I flipped the page over to see if there was a PS on the other side, but that was it. She hadn't even signed her name.

I went to the nearest window and peered out, searching for birds in trees or circling the skies.

The door behind me opened and Davenport came back in.

"My mother lived here?" I took a few steps closer to him and held the letter out, but he skirted around me like I might have an illness he didn't want to contract.

He cleared his throat. "If your aunt says she lived here I'm assuming she probably did. Harriet was not one to make up stories or lie."

I didn't think Aunt Harriet had made that up, but I did start to question whether or not I actually was the right Monica.

"She says I have to feed the garden." I held the letter out again. "Does she mean water? Fertilizer? The garden is already dead. Am I too late?" The desperation in my voice made me realized I really would do anything to stay in this house where it was clean and warm and safe.

Davenport shook his head, a grim line on his mouth. Frustration crept in. Why wouldn't he say anything?

Finally, he opened his mouth and said, "As the letter says, the vultures will show you." He motioned toward the door, dismissing me with a sweep of his hand.

I went up to the rooftop balcony and turned a slow circle. There on the western edge of the property black shapes sat in the trees like garbage bags caught in the branches. One of them took flight, diving down and disappearing into the brush below.

I left through the back door in the kitchen, giving Percy the cook a wave on my way out. I strode across the grounds toward the vultures. They hunkered in the treetops, pink heads nestled between inky black shoulders. They watched me from their perches high above. I found a path hidden in the bushes and pushed through, snapping the small branches on the lower shrubs until I came to a clearing.

A vulture hopped once and flew up into the trees. A few more joined it, swooping in on vortexes and landing. Their feathers rubbed together.

The plot of dirt wasn't big. It was probably fifteen by fifteen feet. The soil looked dry. Placed sporadically on top were rounded stones, like tiny domes had erupted from the soil. They were about the size of cantaloupes.

Rocks? Was Aunt Harriet kidding? What do you feed rocks?

I scoffed, but frowned. My mother's story came to my mind.

There was a little girl…she tended a garden of stones.

Had my mother tended this stone garden? Aunt Harriet's letter basically said she had, and she hadn't liked it.

A breeze swept through the clearing, and with it came the unmistakable scent of rot. Not just any rot. *Death*-like rot. I'd smelled this smell before when one of the old bums who lived in the alley I had to walk through every night died. No one knew he had died—he didn't have a family either, no one to notice he wasn't around anymore—until the smell of him permeated the narrow space between the buildings.

This was that same smell.

I covered my mouth and nose. One of the vultures swooped down and landed among the stones. It hopped once toward a stone that had something encrusted on the top of it, seemed to eyeball whatever the thing was.

The stone shifted.

I let out a strangled cry and backed away. The dirt around the stone crumbled. The vulture jumped backward with a flap of mighty wings. Its clawed foot landed on top of another stone. That stone erupted from the ground exposing a face with sightless eyes and gnashing teeth. Bile rose in my throat. Teeth snapped. The head lunged forward, extending on a too-long neck. It caught the vulture's leg in its teeth.

The vulture fought back, pecking at the head until the teeth released it.

By then, the other stones had begun to move. Not just the nearest ones, all of them. Soft moans came from them, dry and rasping.

"What the hell is this?" I whispered, my voice stuck in my throat. I backed into something and spun around.

Davenport. He took a step back, holding his hands up as if afraid to touch me.

"This is the garden," he said. "The one you must feed."

"But...what...what are they?" They looked human, but they couldn't be. Not with that gray pallor, all bald, eyes... well, I hadn't really seen their eyes, but I knew they had them. Their teeth looked like normal human teeth, too, when the one snapped and grabbed the vulture.

"They are your family."

I looked up at Davenport to see if he was joking. He wasn't. Something told me he wasn't much of a joker.

Family. I should have been horrified. But the truth was, ever since my mom died, I'd always wanted a family. Not like a husband and 2.5 kids. A mom, a dad. Siblings, cousins. I'd been alone since I was five. Old enough for the loss of my mom to hurt forever. The abandonment, even though it was by death and not a decision she'd made.

Hadn't she made the decision, though? To use drugs until it killed her?

"Is she here?" I asked, motioning to the garden. "My mom?"

Davenport's shoulders lifted and fell. He had no other answers.

I didn't know either. Surely there would have been far more *stones* in the plot if it was everyone in my family. I stared out at the mounds, each one representing someone I was related to. The one that had snapped at the vulture had settled back underground, once again a matching dome. The only change was the dirt around them had been disturbed.

I should have been disturbed. But I wasn't. I was fascinated.

They all looked the same. If she was here, how would I ever find my mother among the identical heads? I'd often dreamed that she hadn't really died. That she just wandered off and something happened. That she had wanted and tried to get back to me. I held onto that hope until I aged out of the system.

The last day I saw her alive she'd held me close. I could still feel the warmth of her arms around me, smell her scent —roses, always roses. Her arms had gone from strong and muscular to nothing but bones.

Then she was gone and I was in a place with a bunch of other kids and the rest is history. No one ever wanted me.

Except Bruno. But that was false want. False love. False

belonging. He only cared about the money I made for him and nothing else.

"What do I feed them?" I asked.

Davenport pulled a small journal from the inside of his jacket.

"You'll find the instructions here. Everything you need to know is in this book."

I took it from him.

"Now, Ms. Everette, I must be going. Here's my card. If any of this becomes too overwhelming, do call."

I took the card and slipped it into my back pocket. Part of me didn't want him to go. He'd been my first contact in this new life.

"Will you be back?" I asked, unable to keep the childlike desperation from my voice. I cleared my throat. He wasn't abandoning me. I wasn't his to abandon.

"I'm afraid not," he said. "Unless you call, of course." His eyes darted past me to the garden and I knew it wasn't an *in case you call and need me*. It was an *in case you call to get out of this*.

I looked at the garden, at the stones—yes, I knew they weren't stones, but I couldn't yet call them heads.

When I turned back, Davenport had already left. I could only just see him through the trees.

"Bye," I croaked, surprised at the emotion clotting my throat. But really, why not? I'd just seen a—what even were they? Zombies?—snap at a vulture and now I had to feed these *things*.

My family.

I stepped closer to the nearest one and crouched down.

"Hello," I whispered. I reached a hand forward. Would

it bite me? I touched the cool round pate of this ancestor's head.

It vibrated and warmed under my touch. It shifted and I jerked back and got the hell out of there.

———

Back in the study, I sat down with the journal and a cup of tea and a plate of cookies Beverly brought up. She gave me the best endearing smiles that warmed my heart and dissolved the chilly fog that seemed to metamorph around me since learning of the garden.

Pages upon pages of Aunt Harriet's neat script handwriting talked about the garden.

All my life I knew not of the garden. Not until my mother's death when Marjorie, the elder of the two of us, took on this family tradition. And then she left.

When I read the name Marjorie, I sucked in a quick breath. Marjorie was my mom.

The passages were full of Harriet's disdain.

I am so tired. I tried feeding them animals. Beef, chickens, rabbits caught in the vegetable garden. They snapped at these creatures and, indeed, devoured them as indicated by the mess the next morning, but became restless. They only want one type of meat.

I tried not feeding the garden, only to find my health suffered as a result. My health declined, and I nearly died. I dreamed of my father, telling me I would die and be just like those in the garden if I didn't keep up with the family tradition.

I kept reading. It was clear throughout the journal that

Aunt Harriet did not want to become a member of the garden.

In another passage she wrote that, once she fed the garden, her health returned immediately.

Maybe Mom hadn't been using drugs then. She'd left the garden, this life, behind and suffered because of it. For what? Why would she want to leave this life of luxury?

I looked around at the room I sat in, the heavy velvet drapes, the dark wood furniture. I pressed myself back into the comfort of the chair I sat in. I would never leave. So why did Mom?

I turned the page and a family tree unfolded in all directions from the center of the book. Some names were crossed out, some were connected with a line of blue ink. I found Aunt Harriet and my mother connected to this line, and my own name. *Unknown* was in place of my father's branch on the tree.

I sat up when it came to me.

"She got pregnant," I whispered. "She got pregnant and didn't *want* this for me. She ran away." I paused. "But she would have died when I was a baby." I looked at the page, eyes unfocused. "I lived here."

I ran out of the room and called for Beverly. I found her dusting the books in the library.

"Beverly," I gripped her arm, "did I live here?"

Beverly grinned and pulled me into a hug. "Yes, yes you did. I didn't want to say... Davenport told me I couldn't say anything to you about it unless you figured it out yourself." She pulled away, stroking my ponytail. "The room you picked, that was yours and your mother's room." She stopped smiling. "I was so sad when she ran away with you." She met my eyes, sparkling. "But now you're here again. Back home with us." She hugged me again.

I wondered, as her arms held me in their matronly warmth, if she knew about the garden.

"Maybe you can tell me about her sometime," I whispered.

"Yes, of course."

Back in the study, I kept reading,

Others in our family's past thought it was a curse, but I dug deeper than they did. As a botanist—

Ah, so Aunt Harriet was a doctor of botany.

I discovered a rare fungus that grows on the grounds. A fungus that is used for certain cancers to stop the tumors from growing. It is a dangerous fungus that afflicts smaller organisms, like ants. It takes over their brains and uses their bodies to spread their spores. The ants die and the fungus lives on.

Ophiocordyceps.

She went on to talk about how a member of our ancestry had been afflicted with what sounded like cervical cancer. She had been pregnant at the time. The doctor used *cordyceps* to treat the cancer, not knowing the fungus would affect the fetus.

Because it was a natural remedy, the doctor felt it was safe for the fetus. The fetus survived and grew to be very old. She was the first to join the garden. The cordyceps *lives in the soil. I've tested it and found traces of it there. I've taken samples of those in the garden and found traces of it there in their skin. I dug beneath the surface and found they are all linked by a common root at the center of the plot.*

Feed one, feed all.

The affliction only affects the females in the bloodline. Those who can certainly pass on the gene to their offspring. This is the way of cordyceps. *It is smart and evolves as needed to survive and spread.*

So many family members, but only the women had this gene. Hence the reason why there weren't so many stones —*people*—in the garden. I folded the family tree back into the book and turned the page. Aunt Harriet's handwriting continued.

The last time I fed the garden, I almost failed. It's a weary business earning someone's trust, only to send them to their death. I try to justify it. I'm technically not the one killing them. I only lead them. They tend to walk into the garden on their own, in awe of the stones.

Even Aunt Harriet called them stones.

I daresay, the moonlight glinting off those bald pates is extraordinary. They practically glow. It's an illusion. The pallor of their skin coupled with the blue light of the full moon. She was amazed. I always turn away before the first snapping bite, but I will never forget their screams, nor the strangled sounds they make, nor the sound of rending flesh and gnashing teeth. I never watch. I have never witnessed how a head alone can take down a full-grown human being.

I stopped reading the journal entries there, sickened. I closed the book, picked up a cookie, and leaned back in the chair. I didn't eat the cookie. I set it back on the plate.

I gazed out the window. That's why Mom left this life for one of scraping by and a small and dingy apartment in a bad part of town. This is why she ran away.

It was people the garden wanted. Only people. I

couldn't go to the butcher and order a side of beef. I had to find people and lure them to the garden.

From the final entry in the book, it sounded like it was during a full moon when they had to be fed, which meant I had to feed them about once a month.

"At least it's not every day," I whispered. A tear dripped down my cheek. I wiped it away, then laughed at myself. The next full moon was two weeks away. Aunt Harriet may have had to earn someone's trust, but I already had a fairly large bank of regulars who came to me weekly—sometimes more—to pay for a night of love, want, belonging.

Not to mention Bruno. I frowned.

Bruno and I had a sordid history. After I aged out of the foster system and landed on the streets with nothing but a small suitcase of my second- and sometimes third-hand clothes, I had no one and no where to go. It would have been nice if I'd known about Aunt Harriet back then. To have someone swoop in fifteen years ago to rescue me would have changed my life in every way.

But it wasn't an unknown aunt back then. It was Bruno who found me. Bruno who took me in. He made me feel welcome and loved. It was all part of his manipulation. He made me who I became, and I don't mean that in a lifted-me-up kind of way. He broke me down and pretended to save me.

It only made sense he would be the first I would lure to the garden.

I asked Carl—the driver—to take me back to the city two weeks later.

"Are you sure you want to return to the city?" Carl asked me, peeking at me in the rearview mirror.

"Yes. I have business there." I didn't meet his eyes in the mirror, but looked out the window at the place where I knew the garden hid behind the brambles and bushes.

It was nearing sunset when Carl pulled into the city. Bruno would be easy to find at this time of day. He kept a predictable schedule. I wondered if he would be relieved to see me at first and then be angry, or if anger was his only emotion.

I had the driver drop me off at my usual corner and wait for me there. He was a good driver. He didn't question what I was doing, what my motives and plans were. Hopefully he wouldn't question the vagabond-looking guy I'd be getting back into the car with.

I found Bruno in his usual place outside the back door of a burlesque bar where some of his other girls worked during the early night. Burlesque wasn't stripping, but it was almost better for some people. The show of flesh with some mystery behind it. You'd be surprised how many men were more riled by that than a full-on strip show. I took a deep breath before stepping into the light. I only had one chance.

I stood in the alley entrance and cleared my throat. He looked up. At first with his usual scowl, but then the ridges on his forehead relaxed and his eyes widened.

"Monica?" His voice was full of amazement, and I smiled.

"Hey, Bruno." I waved from the alley entrance, too wary to get within slapping range.

"Where the hell have you been?" He came closer and I backed away. Surprisingly, he stopped. "What are these clothes? Did you buy those with *my* money?"

"No, Bruno. A lot has happened in the past few weeks. Come with me and I'll tell you all about it."

"Come with you where?" His scowl reached his voice. So mistrusting.

"To my aunt's mansion."

I could almost hear the cha-ching in his head and wouldn't have been surprised if dollar signs flashed in his eyes. A leery look came over his face.

"You have an aunt?" Disbelief now. I expected that. Why would I have been with him if I had an aunt?

"She left me everything in her will."

"Everything?"

"Money, Bruno. I can pay you back for everything I owe you and get out of your hair, but you have to come with me."

"Why can't you just bring me the money? Where is this mansion, anyway? I have shit to do tonight."

I ventured a few steps closer. I touched his arm. "I can get you out of this life, Bru."

He looked at my hand on his arm, then down into my eyes.

"You helped me all those years ago. Let me repay the favor?" I hated that I'd pitched my voice softer. It was the voice I used to seduce men. I was pretty enough, I thought, and Bruno thought too, that's why he was so pleased to have me on his "team."

I touched his cheek. He grabbed my wrist and squeezed it hard, then wrenched my arm behind my back and pulled me against him.

"Listen to me, Monica. You don't own me and you never will. I own you. And if you ever think—"

I rammed my heel into the top of his foot. He cried out and released me. I backed away from him and took off at a sprint. This wasn't my plan. Not at all. But when things go sideways you improvise.

Bruno didn't like being hurt—whether it was his pride or physical pain. Naturally, he took chase. My new plan was to get back to the car and as I sprinted as fast as I could, I wondered if the driver would help me wrestle Bruno into the trunk.

I fell against the driver's side door of the car. "Pop the trunk," I called through the glass.

Carl did as told, and I ran to the back of the car. I turned and stood in front of the gaping mouth of the trunk and when Bruno grabbed me, I twisted. His momentum and the movement of my body sent him off balance. He fell into the trunk. I slammed the door on his legs over and over until he pulled them inside himself. He pounded on the inside of the trunk lid.

I hurried around to the back door and got in.

"Back to the house, please," I called to Carl. Bruno's yells came through the seat. His pounding fists.

My hands shook and my heart raced. Bruno's angry cussing and yelling turned to whimpering pleas.

"I'm sorry, Monica. I'll never hurt you again. Please let me out."

Thirty minutes later, I asked the driver to drive out

onto the grounds. He did as told without question. At the hidden passage to the garden, I got out and went to the trunk.

What now, Monica? I wondered. If I opened it and he was passed out or dead, I'd have to drag him into the woods. The driver would see. Did he know the family's secret?

On the other hand, if Bruno was awake and alive, he might come out fists swinging.

I preferred the first option, to be honest. I took a few steps away from the trunk.

"Pop the trunk," I called to the driver. The trunk popped open and Bruno jumped out, but his legs, battered from the beating I'd given them with the trunk lid, wouldn't hold him. He fell onto his knees.

"Goddammit, Monica." He lunged toward me, fell onto his hands, lifted his eyes, and they went wide. He gazed past me, over my shoulder. I turned to see what he was looking at.

The mansion behind me. With windows lit against the dark it really was impressive.

His eyes took in the estate in the blue glow of the full moon. "Oh shit...you weren't kidding." He looked at me, over my shoulder again at the house, back at me. "Are you rich now?"

I cleared my throat and squared my shoulders. "Follow me. I have something to show you." I risked walking right past him. Part of me expected him to grab me, the other part hoped beyond hope he would just do as I said.

He got to his feet and limped after me. I let out a breath.

"How much money do you have now?" He spat the words.

I shrugged. "Enough to live on."

"So you think you can just quit on me, then?" He grabbed my wrist. I stopped walking and turned to him.

"No," I said. "I know I owe you. I'll pay my debts, don't worry." I gave him a coy smile, twisted my wrist out of his grasp, and took his hand. "I'll pay my debts and then some. You can live comfortably. Oh! I know!" I raised my eyebrows and pitched my voice toward excited Valley girl. "Bruno! You could come stay here, with me. Get off the street, out of the life of crime."

I could see the dollar signs flashing in his eyes and a smile played at the corner of his mouth.

"But come here first. You're going to love this." I pulled on his hand and he stumbled along. I pushed through the brush, holding the flexible branches aside while he came through behind me. When we entered the clearing, the sight truly was magnificent.

The full moon glowed on the stones. Aunt Harriet said it was an illusion, but it honest to God looked as if they were glowing from an interior light. Bioluminescent.

"What is this?" Bruno asked. He limped forward past me. Two more steps and he'd be near the first stone at the edge of the plot. He gazed around at them in wonder. One more step.

The first stone shifted. I winced thinking he'd jump back and away.

"What are these things?" He took the last step, crouched low, touched one.

The head lunged out of the earth and snatched his hand in its teeth.

Unlike Aunt Harriet, I did not turn away. The other stones shifted and moved, restless, knowing a feast was coming. They were a single organism. The message of the first stone, that food was here, traveled through their roots, signaling the others. It was beautiful to see them glowing in the moonlight shifting and moving as the message spread.

I thought perhaps it was how they evolved, in case the food got away, they would all be prepared to attack from their long stalk-like necks.

The stone behind Bruno lashed out and caught him on the ankle. It tore his Achilles tendon. Bruno fell over onto his side. The others nearby went in for their own bites, found purchase, tore at Bruno's clothes and flesh.

When he stopped screaming, when he stopped whimpering and begging for me to make it stop, I walked into the stones and pushed parts of him around for the others to eat, though I knew they were all nourished even if only one mouth fed. That's how it worked with organisms like this.

I left the garden when there was little of him left and the stones had settled again. The sky lightened from the inky darkness of night to the pale blue of morning.

Beverly met me in the entry. My shaking hands were covered in blood and dirt. My clothes, too. I let out a whimper. Not because of what I'd seen or done, but because I was free. Truly free.

"I'll run you a bath," Beverly said.

Months later, I toiled in the soil around the stones, cleaning up the mess they'd left from the night before, scraps I would throw to the vultures. I looked around and smiled.

"There was a girl," I said in a low and quiet voice. "She tended a garden of stones." I raked circles around one of the stones like a Zen garden, and really, it calmed me. "A man walked by every day and noticed her toiling away at the dirt, but nothing ever grew." I crouched down next to the nearest stone. "One day, he finally asked her, little girl, what are you doing?" I reached a hand out, stroked the bald pate. "Sir, the little girl said. I'm taking care of my family."

The stone warmed and vibrated against my palm.

Hiccups

HICCUPS

It started with a bad case of the hiccups that lasted for days on end. After the hiccups subsided, the respiratory distress began. Rasping. Wheezing. The hiccups sometimes came back, adding to the patient's distress, but mostly the struggle for breath is what caused the most suffering.

The doctors didn't know what to do. They'd never seen anything like it. It was bronchitis without the cough. Just deep rattling in the lungs. No tumors or growths. Just the rasping.

The first patient to present with these symptoms was given an inhaler, which seemed to help at first. Until it didn't. She had to be sedated and intubated. Even with the sedation she fought. She clawed and gnashed her teeth. It took five to hold her down, to keep her from struggling.

"Fifty more cc's of sedative," the doctor shouted. The nearest nurse who wasn't holding her down administered the sedative straight into her IV, but in the struggle the IV had been ripped out. The fluid dripped onto the floor, wasted.

They finally got her settled and breathing with help from a ventilator.

Another person came in with hiccups. Then another. Three days and five days respectively. Another came in and topped them all. Ten days.

While the new patients got checked in and admitted, the woman on the ventilator sat up and pulled the tube from her throat. She pulled her IV out, removed the heart monitor patches from her chest. She stood and walked out of her room.

The first nurse who saw her dropped the record she was holding and rushed to the patient's side. The patient lashed out. Bit her on the cheek. The nurse screamed and stumbled away. Another nurse came to assist. He also got a nasty bite, but he got the patient restrained at least. Together the two nurses put her back in her room. They used restraints on her wrists and ankles. She struggled, chest heaving, lungs rasping, teeth gnashing.

"There's no way we can intubate her in this agitated state," the doctor said. "Give her a sedative."

"We already did," the female nurse said, touching her bitten cheek. The skin had only broken a little. Probably where the patient's canine hit the soft flesh of her cheek. The male nurse's hand had a full set of teeth indentations. The doctor thought one might be able to make a dental impression from it.

"Get your wounds cleaned up," he said. "I'll take care of her."

The nurses cleaned and bandaged each other up. While they left the exam room they'd used to fix each other, they both started hiccuping.

She laughed and covered her mouth at how loud hers were. He looked at her, worried, and gave her a nervous chuckle in response.

The patient died.

This was how it started. It started with hiccups. It progressed to rasping. It turned to biting. It spread through saliva. It became airborne. There was no escaping it. The hospital went under quarantine. No more admittances. No one could leave. People with incurable hiccups pounded on the doors. Rasped at the windows with the progressed state of the illness.

"Let us in! We're sick!" they called. The doctors, at odds with the oaths they'd taken, turned away, diaphragms spasming with their own case of the hiccups.

The patient lived again. She wandered the halls.

Had it been a mistake? Had she always been alive? Who checked her pulse?

But something wasn't quite right about her. Something just wasn't quite right.

<u>Love At First Sit</u>

STUCK

The chair sat out front on the curb. The old woman's sons, the old woman who had lovingly sat on the chair for the past many years, had carried it out early in the day. The old woman hadn't even said goodbye, and the chair knew it was goodbye.

"Mom loved this old chair. I don't know why." One son placed a sign on the chair's seat. The chair knew what the sign said. It said, "free." Just free. Not "free to a pleasant home." Not "free to a loving family." Not "free to someone who will care and knit arm warmers."

The sons didn't care who took the chair, and it wasn't the first time it had been cast away. Worn leather skin, creaky springs. The lever to recline no longer worked right and needed to be jimmied around a little before the footrest sprang up like a jack-in-the-box. The old woman jimmied it just right every time.

The chair knew about jack-in-the-boxes because it lived with a little baby once. A baby who left marks and stains and smells everywhere he went. He left things sticky, including the chair's arms.

The old woman took the chair in. She wasn't as old back then. She cleaned it up, gave it new life, sat in it every day while knitting and humming and drinking tea and watching her programs, gasping, sobbing, laughing. She had knitted little covers to keep the chair's arms warm, and a hat that lay across the back of the headrest.

The chair relaxed into that life. It loved the old woman.

She had rested in the chair for a few days, unmoving, before the sons came in and found her. Other people carted her off in a black bag. The chair thought they were taking the old woman to be reupholstered. Her upholstery had turned a strange pale color. Sickly and gray.

By then, the chair's upholstery—not real leather by any means, the chair knew—had worn away in the places where the old woman's arms had rested, where her hands had gripped to pull her frail self up, where they had lovingly caressed the chair during her programs.

On the curb, the sky overhead rumbled, threatening rain. The chair hoped the sky would remain closed. To be drenched would be a death sentence. No one would want it then.

A dog on a leash sniffed the chair. Sniffed its little rounded leg stumps and the footrest where the old woman's feet had rested all those years.

The chair knew about dogs. The house with the baby also had a dog. It had lifted its leg on the chair once, leaving a wet spot. The baby's mom had yelled at the dog while spraying the chair with a cleaner of some sort.

This dog sniff-snuffle-sniffed and positioned itself, but a

sharp tug on its leash interrupted it. It went on its way, trotting down the sidewalk. The chair relaxed.

A gust of wind tipped the sign over. The sun came out.

A big, red, noisy pickup truck pulled up. A man and a woman climbed out. They looked at the chair. He lifted the sign.

"Free! Would ya look at that, Bets?" He sat and stroked the worn arms, plucked at some of the peeling not-leather. "Not bad. Not bad." He reached toward the lever and pulled it just right. The footrest sprang up, lurching him back into a more relaxed pose. He snuggled his butt against the chair's springs. "Oh yeah, this is nice, Betsy. This is real nice."

The chair wished it could wrap its arms around him, this man who seemed to love the chair at first sit. He pressed the footrest back inside the chair and got up, the warmth of him dissipating immediately.

"Help me load it up," the man said. The woman, Betsy, looked at the chair.

"Looks a little old, don't it?" She had a sour look on her face. "Probably got peed on or somethin'."

The chair did not like this woman. Did not like the way she looked at it with that yucky face like someone had peed on *her*.

"Yeah, but it's comfy. And it's going in my man cave, anyway. You won't ever see it." He guided her over. "Have a sit down."

The chair wished it could pull back as her ample bottom lowered onto it. The springs creaked and groaned. She leaned back and reached for the lever. She didn't pull it just right. The footrest didn't kick up.

"It's busted, Sam, see?" She jerked and yanked on the handle.

The chair panicked. If she broke it—the footrest released with a *sproing* of springs and cables. Betsy shot back.

No, the chair did not like her. The chair liked Sam.

"Ain't it comfy?" Sam asked, moving closer to stand beside them. He rested his hand on the chair's headrest.

Betsy ground her butt against the chair, shifted around, sat up. "Nah." She climbed out of the chair with Sam's help. They both looked at it.

"I like it," Sam said. "I think it's perfect for my man cave. 'Sides, it's free."

"It's ugly and uncomfortable. We can find better." Betsy climbed back into the truck, but Sam stayed a minute. Sat again. Rubbed his hands over the worn fake leather.

"You're a good chair," he said in a low voice. "But my wife don't think so." He patted the arms, gripped them, and pulled himself up. Just like the old woman had.

He walked around to the driver's side and, with one last look, climbed in and drove off with the roaring, rumbling grumble of the truck's engine.

Days went by. No one else sat on the chair.

A group of kids walked by. The chair knew about kids. The baby and the dog had had an older brother. He and his friends destroyed the rug in the chair's room at that house. Ground orange chip dust into it.

"Ew, who wants someone's gross old chair?" one of them said, kicking the chair's round stumpy leg.

"A cat probably pissed all over it. That's why they don't want it anymore," another kid said.

"No, probably had *kittens* all over it. Afterbirth."

"Eeeew." They got in a pushing fight and ran off.

The chair relaxed.

It sat on the curb, unloved and unwanted.

A few more days went by. One of the old woman's sons came over and dragged the trash cans out. They were full of the old woman's things, including the chair's knitted arm warmers and hat. He put the trash cans right next to the chair, as if he wanted the trash people to believe the chair was also trash.

All the chair could do was sit there looking old and worn and forlorn among the overflowing trash cans.

The rumble of an engine. The trash truck came around the corner. It was five houses away. It stopped. The trash man positioned the can in front of an extendable arm. A pair of prongs grabbed one can, gripped it, lifted it, and tossed the trash into the truck. It lowered the can back to the curb and moved on to the next house. Four houses away.

Same deal. Position the can. Prongs. Toss the trash. Lower the can. Move on.

Three houses away. Prongs. Toss. Lower. Move.

Two. Prongs. Toss. Lower. Move.

One. Prongs. Toss—

There was no one else out. No one to stop these men from allowing the garbage truck to prongs-toss the chair. There would be no lowering.

The truck pulled up to the curb. The man positioned the nearest trash can. The prongs gripped it. One of the knitted arm warmers fell out when the arm tossed the trash inside the truck. It lowered the can. The garbage man moved the other can in front of the prongs. Toss. Lower.

"Should we load this guy in there, too?" the trash collector called, hand on the chair's arm. The chair didn't like this hand. It was dirty and stank of garbage.

The other garbage man came around and scratched his head.

"I mean, we're not really supposed to pick that shit up, but I suppose we could help them out." He looked past the chair at the house. "I think it's an old lady who lives here." He shrugged.

"See if we can lift it with that," the other one said, nodding to the prongs.

They shifted and shoved the chair into position. The prongs came closer. There was no way they would fit around the chair. It was too wide. A foot away, half a foot, inches.

A roaring, rumbling grumble of a truck's engine turned onto the street. *Sam's* truck's engine. The red pickup tore down the street and came to a screeching halt behind the garbage truck. Sam burst out.

"Wait!" Sam called. "I want that chair!"

The prongs, which definitely would not have fit around the chair, pressed into its front, promising disaster to its seat had Sam not arrived.

"Just in time, friend." The garbage guy backed the prongs away from the chair and helped Sam load the chair into the back of Sam's truck. He lovingly draped straps over the chair and cranked them tight, like a supportive hug. He didn't roar and rumble away like he had the first day, but drove slowly, taking the turns carefully. The chair knew it was for it. Sam didn't want it to get hurt.

Nestled into a corner in Sam's man cave, the chair relaxed into a new life. Sam sat in it every morning with a book and his coffee, and every night with a small portion of bourbon and YouTube videos—the chair loved Sam's laugh—until Betsy called him to dinner. Then the chair sat in darkness. But it was safe and dry and someone loved it. That was enough for the chair.

A few weeks into the chair's stay in its new home, Betsy came into the man cave with a vacuum cleaner. She plugged it in and gave the chair a dirty look.

"Falling apart piece of shit," she said. She puttered around the room, straightening up. She ran the vacuum over the rug. The chair wondered if she also hated the rug. It was equally worn and threadbare in places.

The chair thought of Sam as the Giver of New Life. The Gifter of Second Chances to old worn things. All the furniture in his cave was scuffed, worn out, chewed on in some cases—the barstools' lower rungs in particular. Even the dartboard, which Sam brought in after the chair, had more holes than board left. But Sam loved it. Even though the darts often fell out, he and his buddies just kept track of where they'd landed. Sam really wanted to get a used pool table.

"It would go right here," he said.

"There ain't enough room in here for a regulation table," his pal Burt said.

"Doesn't hafta be regulation." Sam pulled out a measuring tape and showed Burt a table would fit.

"It'd be tight," Burt said.

"Like a frog's ass," Sam said.

"I didn't say *water* tight," Burt said, but laughed anyway. The chair liked Burt. He accepted all the old things, and he was a friend of Sam's, so he was a friend of the chair's.

Some nights, after dinner, Sam came back into the man cave and sat on the chair with his bourbon. He nestled down into it, patted its worn arms.

"It's a good chair," he said in a low voice, and the chair knew those words were just for it.

Betsy was in the man cave again. It must have been hot in the main house because she wore short, cut-off shorts and a tank top that left very little to the imagination. Even for a chair.

She looked around at all the worn old furniture and sucked her teeth. The chair didn't like that sound, nor the look—that same yucky sour look—on her face. She moved over to the chair and kicked its stumpy leg.

"Stupid chair. He loves bein' with you more'n bein' with me." She had her hands on her hips. "What's the big deal? You weren't even *that* comfortable."

Then, to the chair's surprise, Betsy sat on it. She nestled down into it with her big heavy butt, jimmied the handle and shot backward.

All of Betsy's exposed upholstery stuck to the chair's fake leather as she shifted around, trying to get comfortable.

"Ugh. So sticky."

Though it felt tacky and damp, her upholstery also felt soft. Supple. Like real leather...but better.

The chair had hoped Sam might reupholster it one day. While it distracted itself from Betsy's shifting and sticking and grunting with thoughts of different fabrics and textures and colors, its fake leather surface grew hot. Maybe from Betsy's warmth, from all the squeaking friction of her skin.

"Shit." Betsy cursed under her breath. "This thing's hot as hell." She peeled her arm up off the chair. Lifted one thigh, then the other, similarly peeling them off. "It's almost...burning." She flailed.

The chair worried she might break it with all the thrashing.

"My arm." She sucked in a breath. "Sam! My arm! It's stuck."

Sam wasn't home. Sam left every weekday morning to go to work after having coffee with the chair. Today was no different.

First one arm. Then the other. The chair latched onto Betsy's soft and supple upholstery. Her thighs stuck next.

Betsy struggled, gasped, and spluttered. She never screamed.

Her thrashing ceased.

Sam came home a few hours later. Betsy's shorts and tank top sat on the chair's seat where they'd fallen, and the chair relished its new upholstery.

"Betsy?" Sam called on his way into the cave. "I'm home. Havin' a beer in the man cave. Shit day at work today." He muttered the last part in the doorway of the man cave. When his eyes landed on the chair, he froze.

The chair didn't know how it looked, but it hoped Sam would like the new upholstery. He moved closer.

"Betsy? Did you get my chair redid?" Sam called over his shoulder. He touched the chair's arm before lifting Betsy's clothes. He grinned and ran off. "Honey, this is amazing! Where are you? In the bedroom?" He let out a lecherous laugh and called her name as he ran out of the cave.

Sam must have thought her discarded clothes were a sign for something. The thing that made the baby in the other house. That had happened on the chair more than once and ended in discarded clothes.

He came back a few minutes later, confusion on his face and Betsy's shorts and tank top in his hands.

The chair yearned for Sam to feel the new upholstery. *Betsy's* upholstery. He had wanted to touch her so badly a minute ago, and now he could. Every time he sat in the chair.

Sam moved toward the chair, turned, and sat.

In Sickness and In Swine

The man at the flea market looked familiar, but Harry couldn't place him right away. There was something in his mannerisms and the way he walked. Something that triggered—not quite a memory—but a feeling of knowing. A reminiscence of a past friendship, perhaps.

Harry followed the man around, ducking under low-slung tents, keeping his eyes on the man's hat. It was a straw cowboy hat with a feather in it. The man stopped at a jelly vendor, picked up a jar, examined it, put it down, nodded to the pretty lady on the other side of the table, and moved on.

At another vendor, the man pulled his other hand out of his pocket to lift a heavy wooden carving. And that's when Harry's memory got jogged. Cold fear spurted into his system, followed by hot adrenaline.

The man's left hand was missing the first and middle fingers.

The memory came at him hard and fast.

Harry had bitten those fingers off.

Two years ago, Harry had been diagnosed with cancer. It had originated in his stomach and spread to other areas of his digestive tract, resulting in the need for a multi-visceral transplant. Harry got a whole new—well, gently used, according to the librarian at the Organ Library—stomach, intestines, and pancreas. His wife, Eliza, who loved him very much, had hocked all of her grandmother's jewelry to help pay for it.

Harry himself had done a stint at the Organ Library for a few months right after college. It was a last resort place to go for this kind of thing, but they were desperate. None of the hospitals around town had a set of viscera ready and waiting. Though he could have undergone treatment for the cancer while waiting, when asked how long that might be, all the surgeons just shrugged their shoulders.

"That's the thing with organs," one of them said. "They don't just show up when you need one. It's not like we have a shelf full of them to pick and choose from." He'd laughed at that, as if sharing an inside joke. But the mention of a shelf of organs reminded Harry about the Organ Library.

Not that it was actually a place with shelves full of organs.

It was a little more sophisticated than that. Mostly.

"I think we need to go to the Organ Library," Harry said to his wife. She looked at him with her tear-reddened eyes, nose pink from blowing it into the multitude of balled-up tissues on every flat surface in their home. She hadn't stopped crying since his diagnosis, despite his assurances that he would be okay. They still had lots of time together and had to make the most of it.

He really wished she would stop crying. That wasn't how he wanted to remember her in whatever afterlife there might be.

When he mentioned the Organ Library and Eliza looked at him, a single tear coursed down her cheek, trembled on her jawline, and fell onto the front of her shirt.

She shook her head. "We can't. We can't." But something had changed in her face. The mask of despair shifted, revealing just a hint of hope in her eyes.

"I hate seeing you like this," Harry said.

She looked at her hands clutching tissues in her lap, and Harry knew she hid renewed tears. He knew she didn't like being a blubbering mess.

In the end, she agreed the Organ Library was where they needed to go to get Harry his new organs.

"You're in luck," the Librarian said. "Just got a fresh set of viscera yesterday. It's clean and healthy. Checked it myself. Couldn't have asked for a fresher set."

The Librarian didn't recognize Harry, and Harry didn't blame him. It had only been three months that he worked there and it was over two decades ago. The man had been old back then, now he was straight up decrepit. Harry assumed one perk of being the Librarian was the first pick of any organs that came in. Extendable life benefits.

"I'll give you a great rate on replacement," the Librarian said. "Half off since you're getting a set of three." He poked at a cash register while he spoke, as if this were a pawn shop running a liquidation sale.

Harry looked at Eliza. She'd already sold all of her grandma's jewelry at this point.

"How much?" she asked.

Harry's surgery and recovery went without difficulty, despite the conditions of the operating room at the Organ Library, or the OR at the OL as the Librarian called it. Eliza had taken to the abbreviation. Harry knew the road to recovery would be long, and he also knew going back to his primary physician for tests and follow-ups would raise eyebrows, so Harry and Eliza found a new doctor for post-op care.

The changes started gradually.

Harry, who had previously loved to eat pork, now had such an aversion to it, his wife couldn't even bring it into the house. The first time she did, he came into the kitchen, nose crinkled.

"What's that smell?" he asked.

Eliza sniffed and shook her head. "I don't smell anything...what does it smell like?"

Harry sniffed the air again. He didn't know how to tell her, but the thought that popped into his mind was, *my brothers*.

"Help me put this stuff away?" she asked. Harry nodded. He opened one of the reusable grocery bags and the smell almost knocked him off his feet. He pulled out a package of pork loins and tossed it across the room. Eliza gave out a cry when the package hit the linoleum floor with a smack.

"That. That's what stinks." He pointed at the offending package face down on the kitchen floor. "We can't have that in the house."

"I was going to make your favorite," Eliza said, retrieving the package.

Harry backed away from her, lifting his hand as if she might attack him with the package of meat.

"Get it out of here," Harry whispered. He turned his head, but watched her from the corner of his eye.

"Maybe I can return it—"

"Just throw it out!" Harry ran from the room.

Meat was out. Harry couldn't stand the sight nor the smell of it. They became vegetarians, and anytime Eliza went out with a friend for lunch, Harry could tell immediately if she'd broken their diet and had meat. She had always loved a Cobb salad. Extra bacon.

Eliza noticed the second change. Harry had always had a little extra hair on his body. His wife loved it. She called it his pelt while lovingly stroking the patch of hair on his lower back or his shoulders.

One evening, while in the throes of passion, she ran her hands across his shoulders and paused.

"You have a...whisker."

"What?" Harry stopped moving his hips and tried to look at where her fingers tickled his shoulder.

"Yeah, or a bristle maybe?" She smoothed her hands over his shoulders. "Oh, here's another one."

Sure enough, Harry had a few hairs on his shoulders that were coarser than the others. After a few months, they tracked across his shoulders and down his back, following his spine.

"I'm disgusting," he said, looking over his shoulder at his back in the mirror.

Eliza ran her hands through his actual—though sparse—pelt. "I love a hairy man," she whispered in his ear, voice husky.

Despite the vegetarian diet, Harry's belly extended beyond the confines of any pants he tried to wear. His first thought was a tumor, so he scheduled an appointment with his doctor to get some tests done. But all the tests came back normal. The doctor ordered an ultrasound, but there was also nothing out of the ordinary there. Harry was perfectly healthy.

"Just try to get some cardiovascular exercise," the doctor said.

Harry nodded. The doctor left the room and Harry wiped the ultrasound jelly from his belly, got dressed, and headed out to the checkout area.

On his way, he heard the doctor's voice say, "Belly like a prize hog, let me tell you. Healthy as a horse, though. Never seen it before in my life."

The last change happened so gradually, Harry only noticed it when he looked back at photos of himself before the surgery.

It was their anniversary, and Eliza always liked to make Harry his favorite—which was no longer her best pork dish, but an assortment of roasted and raw vegetables smothered in butter—and look at their wedding album.

It was his ears he noticed in the pictures. Perfectly

rounded at the tops. He knew they didn't look that way anymore and had chalked it up to the fact that ears and noses keep growing. It was the whole reason old men had such big ears.

But this was different. He jumped up from the table and ran to the nearest mirror.

His once rounded ears now had a slight, almost triangular shape.

"Look at this," Harry said, showing Eliza. "Look at my ears."

She shrugged it off. "Ears keep growing."

"That's what I thought at first, too, but do they change shape this drastically? And over, what's it been, two years?"

"Two years since what?" Eliza was unaware of Harry's calculations.

"Since my surgery," he said.

She batted his arm with the back of her hand. "Don't be crazy, Harry. I don't think ear shape changes are a side effect of having your organs replaced." She laughed it off with her jingling laugh he loved.

That night, while celebrating their anniversary in the bedroom, Eliza ran her hands down Harry's back, now covered in bristling hair. He cringed at her touch, but she claimed she loved how hairy he'd gotten, so he tolerated it. If he was honest with himself, he didn't like her touching him at all anymore. He felt disgusting with his distended belly between them, her fingers running through his pelt...

Sometimes when she came home, he scurried away and hid in the bathroom until she knocked to ask if everything was okay in there. He would come out, feeling sheepish that he hid from his wife, and they would embrace.

Back in the bedroom, Harry whispered, "I don't know how you still love me."

Her hands stopped their exploration of his bristled back, and her eyes popped open.

"What do you mean?" Eliza asked.

Harry rolled off her, no longer in the mood anyway, feeling the way he did.

"Look at this," he said, motioning to his big round belly. "Despite all the running I've been doing, I can't get rid of this."

"Harry," Eliza said. "I married the man, not the body."

That did *not* make him feel *any* better. All it did was tell him she didn't love his body. It was probably why she kept her eyes closed when they came together in marital bliss.

Harry covered his face with his hands, and to his horror, she ran her hand over his belly. His skin tried to pull away from her, twitching at her touch. He leaped out of bed and ran to the bathroom at the opposite end of the house, where he slammed the door, locked it, and backed away. He looked at himself in the mirror. The low light from the nightlight made his eyes look small and black. His pointed ears, now with tufts of bristly fur growing out of them, gave him the horrific appearance of a roasted hog's head on a platter.

He switched on the light and sighed with relief when his own visage appeared in the mirror. He splashed cold water on his face.

A gentle knock came at the door.

"Harry?" Eliza's voice questioned. "I'm sorry... I realize what I said probably wasn't as kind...or comforting...as I thought."

He shook his head. No. It wasn't. All it did was confirm he was a gross, disgusting pig.

"Come to bed, Harry, please?"

He didn't answer.

"You know I love you, Harry. No matter what. It's in our vows. It's in my heart. I sold all of my grandmother's jewelry to keep you here with me. Doesn't that count for anything?"

Harry stared at the door, imagining Eliza's pleading face. How this wasn't the first time she said the wrong thing. She was prone to foot-in-mouth disease and, once upon a time, it had been one of the things he loved about her. Watching her backpedal and try to explain what she actually meant. He knew she didn't say things to hurt him on purpose, and yet, here he was, staring down at his enormous belly, wondering if she really did love the coarse pelt growing on his back and now his front.

"It's our anniversary, please," she pleaded.

He opened the door and there she stood with her own sheepish face. He opened his arms in forgiveness.

***

The following Sunday was their monthly trip to the flea market, which was so much more than a typical flea market. It was almost like a street market in Mexico, with tents and awnings and vendors hocking their locally artisan-ed goods. There were even meat vendors touting their steak burgers and beef sausages.

Eliza tasted samples of all the meat while Harry

pretended not to notice the look of ecstasy on her face when the greasy products hit her tongue.

He left her in the meat section and perused the produce stands, breathing in the earthy vegetable smells.

That's when he saw the man in the straw cowboy hat with the feather sticking out of it and started following him, trying to place him, and when he saw the missing fingers, that's when the memory struck him.

Fear everywhere. The smell of it. The taste of it. It mixed with the metallic scent of blood. Madness surrounded everything. Chaos. They ran down the channels and into a chamber ahead of him. All of his brothers shrieking. Their fear thick around them.

He didn't want to follow them, but their fear carried him in the same direction. At the last moment, he halted. Something struck his backside, but he did not budge from this spot.

A hand reached in. He snapped. Blood filled his mouth. He crunched on the things in his mouth while a human's screams joined the panic of his brothers.

"Get it out of there," someone yelled. More chaos.

He was wrangled and wrestled into a pen, separated from his brothers who were now in the chamber, still screaming, still shrieking.

The man with the straw hat with the feather came in, hand wrapped in a blood-soaked towel.

There was a flash and nothing more.

Harry came out of the memory with sweat soaking his shirt as if he'd run three miles in the midday heat. Everything in the flea market felt too close. Too loud. Too much. He hadn't only bitten the fingers off. He'd eaten them.

The man in the straw hat turned to Harry.

"You okay, son?" he asked. His shirt had a patch on the breast that read Billhilly Farms. It had a round pink pig under the blocky letters.

Harry backed away, eyes darting to the man's hand, to his face, to his hand. Harry turned and ran. He found Eliza enjoying a bite of sausage from a Polish sausage vendor. He grabbed her arm and pulled her out of the flea market and into the daylight, where he gulped lungfuls of air before doubling over and throwing up on the dirt lot. Darkness closed in around the edges of his vision.

"Harry?" Eliza's voice, full of panic.

"Everything okay, ma'am? Sir?" It was the straw hat man. Harry recognized his boots from the memory.

"What happened?" Harry gasped. He righted himself. "What happened to the pig who took your fingers?" he managed to ask.

"How did you know—"

Harry gripped the man's shirt. "What happened to the pig?"

"Harry!" Eliza cried. She pulled on his arm, but Harry kept his grip.

"I shot it. Couldn't send a pig who'd tasted human flesh off to slaughter, now could I? Highly unethical."

"Then what?"

The man let out a nervous laugh, looked at Eliza, then at Harry.

"I left it for the boys on the ranch to deal with. What's this all about, son?" The man touched Harry's hand.

Harry loosened his grip and let the man go. Eliza pulled him away.

"I'm so sorry, sir," she said as she guided Harry to their car. They got in. "Jesus, Harry. What were you thinking? You assaulted that man."

"He killed me," Harry whispered. "I ate his fingers and he killed me." He looked at her face, full of worry.

"What—I don't—What?" Her voice had raised a few octaves. Harry could smell the meat on her breath. It soured his stomach.

His *pig* stomach. *Swine. Hog.*

"It explains everything." He ran his hands over his belly. "This. The fur. My ears. My diet and appetite."

"What explains everything? I'm not following you." Eliza had tears in her eyes now. "I'm worried about you, Harry."

"Take me to the Organ Library."

"The Organ—"

"Just take me, Eliza. Trust me." He strapped on his seat belt.

She started the car and in forty-five minutes, pulled up at the Organ Library.

"Stay here." Harry ran inside. The Librarian looked up from an enormous book spread out on the counter. "Do you keep track of where the organs come from? Do you know where they come from when people bring them in?"

"Calm down, sonny boy," the Librarian said. "I sometimes know. Sometimes don't ask. What's it to ya?"

"You may not remember me, but around two years ago I came in looking for a stomach, intestines, and a pancreas, and you delivered."

"Okay...and? Something not working out for ya?" His lascivious eyes raked over Harry's distended abdomen, and Harry self-consciously covered his belly with his arms. "Where did you get those organs?" Harry asked.

"The usual places. A Librarian doesn't tell his secrets."

Harry jabbed a finger at the Librarian, who didn't flinch.

"I think they were pig organs you gave me. *Pig*." Spittle flew from his mouth, speckling the Librarian's glasses.

The old man did not have fear in his eyes, nor did he smell like it. He chuckled.

"Now, what gives you that idea?"

Harry stripped off his shirt and showed the man his back. He wiggled his ears, which had grown so large, the pointed ends had flopped over on themselves. He squealed, and it sounded exactly like a pig. He told the Librarian about his aversion to meat products, his diet of vegetables, how *this* happened despite only eating vegetables. He said this last while pointing at his big round belly.

"I'm turning into a goddamn *pig*."

The door behind him opened. "Harry?" Eliza's voice asked, quiet, tentative, *frightened*.

Harry spun around with a grunt. Not just a grunt. A snort. An *oink*. He covered his mouth and rushed toward Eliza, shoved past her out into the late afternoon sun. Tears poured down his cheeks as he ran. Instead of sobs, heart-wrenching squeals belted from his windpipes.

Jesus Christ, he thought. *I'm wee-wee-wee-ing all the way home.*

That's when he stopped and placed a hand against a brick building to catch his breath. He peered in the darkened shop window at his reflection. His ears, the bristles spilling out of the collar of his shirt. He turned his head this way and that, taking in his changing appearance.

Was his nose slightly turned up at the end now? Were his cheeks more expansive? He grinned at his reflection, checking his teeth.

Their car rolled up against the curb behind him. He watched Eliza lean over the center console.

"Harry, get in the car."

"I'm a monster," he whispered.

"Get in now." Eliza's voice held uncharacteristic anger. He turned and slid into the passenger seat. Eliza gripped the wheel.

"What was that back there? Huh? What is going on?"

"I'm turning into a pig," Harry said, weeping. "I think those boys at that farmer's farm took the pig organs to the Organ Library." His voice came out a boy's punished tone, low and quiet and ashamed. He wrung his hands. They still looked like human hands. For now.

Eliza sighed. Her hands fell from the steering wheel. She shifted in her seat to face him. He continued to stare at his hands. Her long narrow fingers slid onto his palm.

"You aren't turning into a pig," she said. But her eyes danced up to the flopping points of his ears, triangulated to his shoulders where the bristles poked through the thin cotton of his shirt. She ran a hand over his cheek. "And even if you are, I'll love you anyway." Eliza leaned forward and kissed him.

Her words didn't make him feel any better. Her love wouldn't turn him back into a full human.

When Eliza had spoken her vows at their wedding, she meant them with all her heart, body, soul, mind, essence, and being. When she told Harry she married the man, not the body, what she meant was she loved Harry for who he was inside, not how he looked on the outside. She had always thought he was a dreamboat.

She wasn't blind to the changes he went through, but she accepted them. She did all she could to prove she loved him despite them. Harry didn't seem to believe her. He scoffed at her and waved her away while sadness filled his eyes.

They could no longer go out in public, but Eliza didn't care. She was happy to do the grocery shopping and pick up whatever he needed. Harry cooked and cleaned. He became a regular old house husband until he could no longer hold the broom because of his hands turning into trotters.

He could still talk, and his eyes were still his eyes, and he was still the man she'd married in mind and soul.

But she hated how these changes affected him emotionally and mentally. How down on himself he was. He was often grumpy—not at her, never at her—but he moped around. She caught him looking at himself in the mirror, quietly weeping at what he'd become.

"You should leave me. Start a new life," he said to her one night while they lay in bed reading. She could still understand him, though his voice had grown gruff and his breathing rattled in and out. Maybe because she'd been with him through the whole change, she had learned to hear him through the other sounds his vocal chords made when he spoke.

"Never, Harry. In sickness and in health, 'til death do us part." She kissed the tip of his snout. "As long as we both shall live."

He snorted at that, and his piggy lips curled up into a smile. She touched his big, round cheek.

"There's that beautiful smile. I've missed it." She kissed his snout again and rolled over.

As Harry's horrendous snores filled the room, Eliza stewed with anger. Not at Harry. Never at Harry. She was mad at the situation, at the events that had led up to this. At herself.

After Harry had run out of the Organ Library those months ago, she had politely asked the Organ Librarian where the organs her husband had received came from. He hemmed and hawed and flipped through his book, consulting its pages.

"I told your husband. A couple of boys brought them in." He scratched his stubbled chin. "If I remember right, they'd come from Billhilly Farms. Had the patches on their jackets. Reeked of pig manure."

Eliza pursed her lips and, with a raised eyebrow, observed the Organ Librarian piece together what he'd just confessed. Watched the lightbulb click on behind his dumb beady eyes.

"I'll be damned," he whispered. "Pig organs."

Eliza had turned and left the Organ Library, found Harry, and took him home. The next few weeks she pored over the contracts and agreements Harry had signed when he had his surgery. He'd apparently signed a nondisclosure agreement which prevented him from going to law enforcement or seeking legal counsel or arbitrary action about anything that happened up to and including acts of God.

She shoved the papers away. Harry was out back foraging in the woods behind their house. He came home with roots and mushrooms and other things he'd acquired a taste for. Grubs and other bugs included. Eliza didn't care, as long as they didn't escape to crawl around the house.

There was nothing they could do. The Organ Library's contracts were watertight.

"Like a frog's ass," Harry whispered when Eliza told him.

"Like a frog's ass," she agreed. "I'm so sorry, Harry."

"What can you do? It's not your fault."

But it was. She'd pushed him to do the surgery, so afraid of losing him too soon. She had to make it up to him.

On a cloudy day in the fall, she drove to the Organ Library and pushed her way inside. The bells on the door jangled, and the Librarian looked up from his massive tome.

"Well, I'll be. The pig man's wife." He chuckled. "How is our little swine these days?"

"You'll never believe it, sir," Eliza said, closing the door behind her gently. "He's completely turned into a full pig. I just don't know what to do! He's not my husband anymore. I wouldn't want to be accused of bestiality or anything unsavory like that." She moved closer to the counter and leaned against it, pressing her bosom together. "Is there anything you can do to help me?"

The Librarian pulled his eyes from her cleavage to her face. "Full pig, eh?" He licked his lips.

Eliza could hear the wheels grinding in his skull, sending messages about fat rashers of bacon to his gut. His stomach growled audibly.

"Would you like to see him?" she asked.

His eyes widened, brightened. He wiped the back of his hand against the corner of his mouth. "Of course I would."

She insisted he ride in her car with him. "No worry at all, I assure you. Happy to drive you over *and* back to the library. The price of gas these days—"

"Hoo-wee, tell me about it. All right. I'll ride with you."

Eliza quietly listened to the Librarian regale her with the things people did to deliver organs.

"One man sewed a foot inside his abdomen. Grossest thing I've ever seen, and you *know* I've seen my share of gross things." He cackled at that.

"You take feet?"

"Feet, legs, hands...the works, really. If it can be sewn on or reattached, I'll take it."

"And you don't test the...um...products when they come in?"

"Nah. I have a trusted pool of donators."

Eliza tried not to frown. *Except for the boys from Billhilly Farms,* she thought. "Here we are," she said as they pulled into the driveway.

The Librarian clapped his hands and rubbed them together while licking his lips. He followed Eliza to the front door, through the house, and out the back. The sun slid toward the horizon, casting everything in a blood-orange glow.

"Harry," Eliza called. "We have company."

The Librarian grunted a laugh. "Heh heh heh." His beady eyes scanned the tree line, but that's not where Harry was.

The door to the shed burst open. The Librarian cried out. "I thought you said he was a full pig."

Harry stalked toward them on his hind legs. The Librarian turned with a frightened cry, but Eliza grabbed him and held him tight. He was bones and flesh and easy to crush against her.

"This is what revenge looks like," she growled in his ear. Harry stood only feet away. "He's all yours, my love."

"Please. I'm sorry. I didn't know." The Librarian cried.

Eliza gripped him tighter. Air wheezed out of his lungs. "That's not what you told me at the Library," she said, eyes locked on Harry's. They were still his eyes, and as long as they were, and as long as they conveyed he was still the man she married, she would be with him. She would keep him and have him and hold him.

The Librarian lifted his hands in futile defense.

Harry started with his fingers.

Bone Curse

THE LAST PERSON ANYONE WOULD EXPECT

Her name was Melanie Last Name Redacted. She was beautiful, or had been, Bethany was sure, when she was alive.

Now she was pale. Her eyes, listed as having been a deep dark brown color, were now gray and clouded over.

"Do you ever wonder who these people were?" Bethany asked her anatomy partner, Jacob.

Jacob, never Jake. She learned that their first day in anatomy together.

He shrugged one shoulder, staying cool and distant as usual. "We are here to dissect her." Jacob pulled on a pair of nitrile gloves. "Not learn her story." All work, all seriousness. He positioned the scalpel over her right biceps.

When their professor assigned them together, Bethany had felt relief. He was the top student in all of his classes—something he didn't brag about, but he didn't have to. Others bragged about him. They called him The Brain.

Bethany's grades had been average, sometimes dipping below average. She just could not get ahead in her studies.

She needed to get a solid grade in this class or else she'd be dismissed. Her academic advisor had been clear about that in a letter she received the previous semester. Her hope was Jacob could help her. But so far, it seemed his only concern was for his own *summa cum laude* status.

Jacob cut into Melanie's arm and flayed open the skin. They were studying limbs. Musculature, nerves, tendons, major arteries, joints. The works.

He got down to the bone—her humerus—and jerked back.

"What is it?" Bethany asked.

"Look at this." He pushed his glassed up his nose with the back of his wrist.

She leaned over and peered past the layers of epidermis, dermis, subcutaneous tissue, and muscle. The bone inside was bright white, in contrast to the dull colors around it. If it hadn't been so bright, they may not have noticed the pale brown etchings along the length of the bone.

"Is that writing?" Bethany asked.

Jacob dropped the scalpel. It clattered onto the metal tray. Sweat broke out on his face, making his skin look waxy. He gripped his chest.

"Jacob?" Bethany screeched when he went down to his knees. He rasped in breath after breath, but his chest didn't seem to rise. Bethany tore off her gloves and dialed for an ambulance.

It didn't arrive in time.

Because of Jacob's death, Bethany's academic advisor told her she automatically passed Human Anatomy Lab. The student bereavement policy allowed her time off to grieve if she needed it.

Jacob's cause of death was myocardial infarction and respiratory failure. Something rarely heard of at his young age, especially in the condition he was in. Bethany had never seen him smoke, drink, or eat anything that wasn't a salad or lean meat. He ran every morning, and she never saw him without a water bottle. He could have been the poster child for good grades *and* good health.

Bethany opted not to take the time away. Even with the automatic pass, she wanted to keep going. She spent a week cutting Melanie open, examining her bones. Every one of them had the strange marks in vertical lines down the length of each bone. She searched for meaning in them. Googling arcane symbols, old languages, ancient character sets, but she wasn't a linguist and had no interest in that kind of thing, and turned her attention back to finding out who Melanie was. The question she'd proposed to Jacob that first day, before he died.

After long, sleepless nights spent scouring the internet for information, she finally found what she was looking for. Melanie's family had donated her body to the school.

Bethany wrote the details in her lab notes: Melanie Fort. Age eighteen. Cause of death: undetermined.

Her parents had not opted for an autopsy. Bethany found that odd, given how young she was.

She found Melanie's obituary as well, jotted down her parents' names—John and Cindy Fort—and, after a quick search, she found them on social media.

They were a nice-looking couple. Photos of Melanie plastered Cindy's feed. John's just had reshares of memes, but his last post was that he was leaving social media to be with his wife during this difficult time.

Bethany wanted to send Cindy a message, but she wasn't sure what to say, nor how to say it. Besides, it would be highly against school protocol to contact the body's next of kin. Her thumb hovered over the message button. She bit her lip and tapped it, and before she could turn back, she typed:

I need to talk to you. It's about Melanie.

Bethany was tired and in desperate need of sleep that wouldn't come to her. She wasn't exactly sure what she even wanted from Melanie's mom. She slid her phone into her pocket just as it vibrated with a response.

Meet me at nine a.m. tomorrow at the cafe on the corner of First and Linfield.

Bethany arrived half an hour early. Nerves made her twitchy and jumpy and her hands wouldn't stop shaking. She had a strange chilly sensation in her core that made her feel trembly all over.

Cindy arrived early, too. She wore large sunglasses that covered most of her face.

"Bethany?" she said, gripping the handle of her handbag with both hands.

"Yes. Are you Cindy?" The woman confirmed, and they shook hands. Cindy took the seat across the little round cafe table. She removed her sunglasses. Her eyes were bloodshot and red-rimmed.

Bethany opened her mouth but didn't know what to say. Her face grew hot. "This is so...um...so inappropriate," Bethany said. "I-I'm sorry to have bothered you." She grabbed her bag, but Cindy stopped her.

"No, please." Cindy's voice cracked. She sniffled and pulled out an overused tissue from her purse. "Please. Stay. Please sit." She dabbed her nostrils.

Bethany sat. Cindy put her sunglasses back on. Bethany could only just see her eyes behind the lenses.

"Did you know my Melanie?" A tear slid out from behind the large frames.

Bethany bit her lip and looked at her lap. "I didn't." She met Cindy's eyes. "I'm a medical student. My partner, Jacob, and I had her...cadaver...in Human Anatomy Lab." She spoke fast. "My partner died seconds after cutting open her arm." Bethany touched her right arm.

Cindy's lip trembled. She took a deep breath and let it out. A server came to their table. She ordered a coffee, but Bethany was too jittery for caffeine. She ordered a muffin and a glass of water, even though she knew she wouldn't eat the muffin.

"I knew we shouldn't have donated her," Cindy said in a low voice. Her lips turned down at the corners. "The school is my husband, John's, alma mater. He was in the pre-med program before he switched gears to become a mechanic. No pun intended."

"Quite a switch," Bethany said. The server dropped off their orders. "Why did he change his mind about medicine?"

Cindy shrugged. "He never told me. Any time I pressed the issue, he got mad, so I guess I just stopped asking."

"Tell me about Melanie," Bethany said. "If you're okay to talk about her."

Cindy nodded. "I can talk about her. I love talking about her. She was smart. Athletic. Kind." Cindy ticked off a list on her fingers. "She was a wonderful daughter. Never moody or angry at us. The rare times she got in trouble, she took her punishment in stride. She was a good girl."

"She was very beautiful," Bethany said. "I saw her pictures on your social media feed."

Cindy smiled shyly and looked at her coffee cup. She twisted it on the table.

"What did your partner...experience—I mean, did he experience anything strange before he died?" Cindy asked. She turned her eyes to Bethany's. "I know...it's a weird question. I'm sorry... You don't have to answer it."

"No, I—it's fine. If you can talk about Melanie, I can talk about him...about something we found."

Cindy nodded and licked her lips, pulling them both inside her mouth.

"He had her humerus exposed and—" Bethany took a deep breath. "She had markings on her bones. All of them. I've gone over her entire body."

"And Jacob? What happened?"

"He stepped back so I could look, and when I turned around, he was pale and sweaty. He fell. He couldn't breathe. His lungs failed and he had a heart attack—"

Cindy's fist hit the table. "Dammit." Her eyes had filled with tears. She blinked them rapidly away while her jaw clenched and unclenched.

"What? What is it? What are the marks? How did they get there?" Bethany gave Cindy a few moments to compose herself.

"This is going to sound crazy," she said in a low voice laced with emotion. "It's the bone curse."

"Bone curse?" Bethany stifled a strong desire to scoff. She cleared her throat. "What is the bone curse?"

"It runs in my family, on my side. The first woman to have it was back during the Salem witch trials. They burned her at the stake. Any male who came in contact with her remains died exactly the way Jacob did." Cindy sucked in a gasping breath and covered her mouth. Her eyes contorted with grief. She got it together. "I'd hoped it would have skipped my Mel, but I knew it all along." She shook her head.

"How did Melanie die?"

"The way any other woman with the bone curse dies, except those burned at the stake. Abruptly and without cause or reason. Just taken. Taken from this world. Taken from those who love them. Doesn't matter their age. When their time comes, they just go."

This all sounded ridiculous. Bethany wondered if this grieving mother hadn't lost her marbles. But at the same time, she believed her.

"You need to close her up. Don't let any other men see her bones. Don't let anyone else touch her body. Get rid of it. Burn it." Cindy's eyes were earnest as she gripped Bethany's hand.

That's why there hadn't been an autopsy, Bethany realized.

"Why donate the body then? If you knew?" She didn't want to get mad about it, but if Cindy knew about the curse—

"It was John," Cindy said. "He insisted. I tried to warn

him, but he didn't believe me." Her face contorted for a split second, but she composed herself. "It caused a lot of strife in our marriage. I relented. Only because I didn't know for sure—" She hitched in a breath, expelled a sob, and covered her mouth with the tattered tissue. "I'm sorry," she whispered.

"I have to go," Bethany said.

Cindy grabbed her wrist. "Be careful," she warned. "The longer her bones are exposed, the stronger the curse gets. It could get you, too."

Melanie's bones had been exposed for over a week, and Bethany had been in the lab with her at every spare moment.

Bethany went straight to the lab to do as Cindy asked, but the table where Melanie had been lying was empty. No body. No Melanie.

A rasping wheeze brought Bethany around the counter. Her professor lay on the floor, gasping for air that wouldn't fill his failed lungs.

"Where is she?" Bethany asked. He pointed. Bethany turned just as Melanie's body—ambulatory and with vicious intent—raised a metal tray and smashed it down onto her head.

Bethany came to with the sound of buzzing or drilling, and the scent of smoke and something else. Someone hummed a tuneless song. A thick grogginess made her eyes slow to open, sensations difficult to comprehend. She was aware of pain and a figure huddled over her arm, long hair creating a curtain, blocking Bethany's forearm and hand.

The woman turned her head. Cloudy eyes met Bethany's. A smile crackled across Melanie's lips.

"Now you'll be like me," the woman's lips said. The words were inside Bethany's head. She lifted Bethany's hand to show her.

The skin lay open, exposing the bones marked with symbols. Melanie held an engraving tool in her other hand.

The Scent of Blood

The room smelled like blood. Every time she took a shower, it just stank of blood in that room.

She'd moved into the house a week ago, enamored by the huge backyard. The house itself was subpar. Outdated cabinets in the original oak popular among the home builders of the '70s. Nothing had been updated.

The previous owner had so much furniture along the edges of every room, she didn't notice anything odd about the house, and once she saw the expansive and private backyard, full of established trees, she put in an offer.

It was a quiet neighborhood. Not because it was by a cemetery, but because they were on a street off a street off a main road. No one but the handful of their neighbors drove on that street.

She didn't notice the smell, because the smell only happened after showering in the upstairs bathroom. The room that ended up smelling was the mechanical room. The mechanical room was in the basement and housed the furnace, hot water heater, and the washer and dryer. It was a dark, claustrophobic little room, and whenever she went in there after her shower, it brought it all back.

The dark closet.

The stench of wool.

The feeling of shoes under her, making her perch, precariously unbalanced, on the floor of the closet.

The every-second-fear that rattled her teeth.

The loud *bang*.

The ensuing silence.

Then the smell.

Metallic. Hot.

Blood.

This was why, after three weeks in that house, she thought about walking away from it. Taking the hit to her credit. But no. She couldn't let the past destroy her present. Besides, maybe she remembered it wrong.

Maybe it didn't happen how she remembered.

She called her sister. Her sister had been there that night, too. Her sister hadn't been in the closet.

"Hey, Dum-Dum," her sister said in answer.

"Do you remember that one night when we were kids when...Dad...uh...died?"

Her sister scoffed. "Yeah."

"What do you remember happening?"

Her sister took a deep breath. "This was not a conversation I was expecting to have today."

"I know. Or ever, right?" She laughed a can-you-believe-this kind of laugh, even though she was the one asking the question. "So? What happened?"

Her sister sighed again. "Mom and Dad were fighting.

Things escalated. He hit her. She—she shot him." Her sister's voice had a shrugging quality to it.

"You're sure?"

Her sister made an affirmative noise. "Why? What do you remember?"

It was her turn now, to take a deep breath and heave a big sigh.

"I remember being in the closet. It was dark. It smelled like that old wool coat Dad always wore in the winter." Her mind went back to that day once again.

Her mom and dad started fighting over something stupid, she was sure. That's what married couples always fought about. Stupid things that don't matter that are probably masking some deep underlying issue, but both are too afraid to dig into what it even was. Of what it might bring to the surface and do to the marriage.

It started with a bickering disagreement, then a voices-raised argument. Then a screaming match.

Her sister ushered her into the closet, shushing her as she closed the doors. Her sister put her away for safekeeping.

Under her feet were the shoes. Dad's stiff leather business shoes, Mom's high heels. They poked at her bare feet and her bottom. She wobbled around, trying to get into a comfortable position.

Her hand found a metal case deep in the back of the closet.

She opened it. In the darkness, her hands touched and fluttered over something cold and metal squeezed into that rough squishy material she'd seen used in packing. She didn't know what this thing was. She was only six. She dug her fingers along the edge and pulled the heavy thing out. With it in her hands, feeling it all over, she knew what it was. Her favorite after-school show had a cowboy in it. It was his trusty pistol.

She was a cowboy now, with *her* trusty pistol.

Things outside the closet had heated. Someone smacked the other. A gasp. It was Mom's gasp. Had she struck Dad, surprising herself, or did Dad strike her, surprising her just the same?

Beyond the door, their screaming voices dropped to lowered harsh whispers. Whisper-yelling at each other. The words must have been too evil for younger ears.

She turned her attention back to her trusty pistol, raised it.

"Reach for the sky," she whispered. Her little fingers pulled at the trigger, but they were too weak. She adjusted her grip on the heavy thing to get more fingers on that trigger. She finally got them positioned.

The bang deafened her. So much louder than the cowboy's gun from her after-school show. All she could hear was a high-pitched tone. She was on her butt at the back of the closet.

A thin stream of light came in through the closet door, boring a hole into the center of one of Mom's red velvet pumps.

Through a mile of cotton, Mom's muffled shouts of Dad's name.

"Mom?" Even her own voice sounded underwater. She squeezed her eyes shut and rubbed at them while stumbling over the shoes to the closet door. At the front, the little dark room smelled metallic.

The thin stream of light wasn't shining on Mom's red pump. It shined on the carpet, saturated with blood. Blood that had seeped in from out there. The other side of the door. The smell of it filled the small room. With her ears underwater and the darkness—save for that stream of light coming in through the new hole in the door—and the smell, she felt a little woozy. She needed air. She stumbled forward, bare foot squelching in the wet carpet. The door wouldn't open. She turned the knob, pushed and pushed. The smell got stronger. She tasted it in the back of her throat.

She pushed and pushed at the door, slipping on the shoes with bloody feet, breaths gasping in and out, short and shallow. It finally budged open enough for her to fit through.

She tumbled out into the cooler air and landed in the puddle. In the blood. It coated her hands and forearms. Slimed the front of her t-shirt.

Dad lay on the ground, blood burbling out of a hole in the side of his neck. Mom shrieked, hovering over him, hands fluttering around at the hole in the side of his neck.

There was a hole. In the side of his neck.

Blood poured out of it.

She, the six-year-old from the closet, held the gun. She had been the one. She had always been the one who shot him.

"That's how I remember it," she said in the here and now on the phone to her sister. "The smell of blood, to this day, brings that memory back to me. I always remember it this way."

Her sister's silence did not come through the line.

"Are you still there?"

"Yeah," her sister said on an exhale. "I'm here."

"Were you there? When it happened?"

"Yeah."

"Do you remember? Me? With the gun?"

"No," she said. "I couldn't see you from where I was standing."

"Where were you?" She didn't remember seeing her sister in the room.

"On the other side of them," her sister said. "With the gun from the bottom drawer of Dad's bedside table."

Dwelling

WHAT IS THAT SMELL?

Dave and Go-Go lived in the Johnsons' attic. Before that it was the Farleys, and before that the McMurphys, and before the McMurphys it was the Gibbons. They had the best leftovers. Always something homemade from scratch.

"Nothing like a home-cooked meal," Dave had said, pulling half a pan of lasagna out of the fridge.

It never ceased to surprise Go-Go how people just didn't remember what they had in their fridges. How often leftovers were thrown out because no one knew when they had eaten that particular meal, and therefore didn't know how old the food was inside.

Except the McMurphys. Ben McMurphy always knew what, when, and how old the leftovers were. He always detected missing leftovers. Dave and Go-Go didn't stay there too long. Ben noticed too much about their food supply and became suspicious. He almost caught them once when he roamed around the house, gun in hand, looking for intruders who had eaten the last single-serving bag of potato chips. His wife called him off at the last second, telling him he was being ridiculous and that *she* had probably eaten the last bag without remembering.

"Why are you so goddamned concerned about the food supply? It's not like we're starving to death."

Ben had been a doomsday prepper. That's why he was so concerned.

When Dave and Go-Go ate anyone's leftovers, they always cleaned up the dishes and put them away. It wouldn't do to leave dirty dishes in the sink when there weren't any there in the first place. Sometimes Go-Go even washed dishes the Johnsons had left in the sink.

"I'm the dish fairy," she said, placing the clean dishes in the dish drainer or filling the dishwasher. It was the least she could do. Her contribution to the household.

Before they started dwelling, they'd been kicked out of the last apartment they'd lived in legally. Go-Go had accidentally set fire to the curtains with her curling iron. She was trying to create a following on YouTube with beauty tips and tricks. The best lighting was by the window and the gauzy curtains gave her videos a certain whimsical look into her otherwise shitty life.

They couldn't find a place that cheap to live afterward —not that anyone would rent to them after that fiasco anyway—and neither one of them could hold a job because neither one of them liked to work for, or wanted to work for, *The Man*.

The idea came to her when they were wandering the streets of a swanky neighborhood. Nice cars, big houses. A black Mercedes C43 AMG pulled out of an enormous slate-blue house with white trim. Go-Go waved as the people drove by, but the driver's face was obscured by a travel coffee mug and the passenger leaned his against the window with his eyes closed.

They forgot to close the garage.

"Let's go in." Go-Go pointed at the open garage. There was the usual accumulation of Colorado life inside. Mountain bikes, kayaks, camping stuff.

Dave, always one to do as Go-Go wished, shrugged one shoulder and grinned. "Okay."

Go-Go ran across the street and into the garage with Dave trailing behind her. She hit the button on the wall and closed the door.

That's how they lived in their first attic. Undetected. Rent-free.

For a year they did this. Moving from place to place, living a week here, a month or more there.

While the homeowners were out at their cushy day jobs and the kids were off to school, they crept into the house, ate from the pantries and refrigerators, and filled their water bottles. If nothing else, they always had water on hand.

Go-Go always crooned over the high-end hair products these women with their expensive hair dye jobs and highlights used.

After learning the owners' schedules, sometimes they even did some laundry. They never stole anything except food. Every once in a while, they would nap in one of the beds or watch TV on the couch. But they always had an ear out for garages opening, cars driving up the street, people coming home.

They'd been in the Johnsons' attic for two weeks.

"I don't want to do this anymore," Dave whispered. "I want to make a life for us."

"What, and work for the man?" Go-Go was taken aback. Dave had never expressed interest in this before. "You don't want to do that. The man will own you."

"Just for a bit, Go. Just to get some money so we don't have to live in secret anymore. I'm tired." He took a deep breath. "I'm scared all the time. Constantly worried we're going to get caught. I don't want to go to jail again."

"We won't get caught." Go-Go silently fumed after this. Dave could go get a job and do whatever the hell he wanted. She was going to keep dwelling. As she thought about what he said, though, she started to realize he wanted to do it for her.

"You want to make a life for us?" she asked in a whisper. "Like, marriage and stuff?"

Dave took her hand. "Yeah. I want to provide for you."

"I don't need a man to provide for me," Go-Go snapped. "But...that's real nice, Dave. I think...I think I might like that."

"I'm so glad, Go. Yesterday when I left for a little bit, I actually got a job at that gas station on the corner. I start in two days." She could hear his excited smile in the darkness of the Johnsons' attic. "I still have a little cash left from that last gig I did. We could stay in that cheap motel where we used to pass all the time before we came to this neighborhood."

"The one that's like two-hundred a week?" she asked.

"Yeah. We could stay there until I get my first check. I bet you anything Bobby'd let us rent a room at his place for a while after that. He could be our reference to get our own place."

Go-Go liked the sound of that. She'd always liked

Dave's friend Bobby. Whenever they saw him and talked about dwelling, Bobby always rolled his eyes and said they could always come stay at his place for cheap if they wanted.

Back then, Go-Go always said no. She liked dwelling. She never had to cook or clean—except the dishes. She got to use the luxury shampoos and conditioners. But now, if she was truly honest with herself, after nearly getting caught by Ben McMurphy, the thrill of dwelling had been tainted. There was that little itch of anxiety under her breastbone every day. She hadn't realized what it was until Dave mentioned it.

"Okay," Go-Go said. "Okay. Tomorrow when the Johnsons leave, we'll get out of here and go to Bobby's."

Dave squeezed her hand. "I'll make you proud, Go. I promise."

But the Johnsons didn't leave the next day. Nor the next.

Go-Go crept across the joists to a vent in the ceiling and listened. She heard snatches of phrases. Words like "global pandemic," and something about Corona. She thought they were talking about beer, but it didn't make sense.

"I'm hungry," Dave whispered when she crept back to him. Their water supply had run low, too. Go-Go knew they could survive without food for a time, but not without water.

"I'll get something to eat," she said.

"You can't. They're home."

She pressed her finger to his lips and shushed him.

Go-Go grabbed one of the cloth bags they used to collect snacks and crept to the attic door, which wasn't a door, but a panel in the floor. She shifted it aside and listened at the crack. Desperate to get Dave something to eat—he'd never gone as hungry as she'd gone before—she dropped down onto the plush carpet and stayed in a crouch, listening hard.

Someone was upstairs in the shower. Someone else was downstairs watching TV. She could hear the unmistakable mumbled rumble and in-between stories musical tones of the news.

Go-Go knew she could sneak down the stairs and into the kitchen undetected. The living room was not visible from any vantage point on the way. In the kitchen, she grabbed an apple from the bowl of fruit on the kitchen bar.

"Shit," Mr. Johnson muttered from the hallway. Go-Go froze, watching his shadow on the wall. It retreated back to the living room. She let out a breath.

The TV blared. Go-Go listened.

The newscaster encouraged people to stay home.

It wasn't beer they were talking about. It was a virus. A global pandemic had swept the world. Deadly. So many people had already died. Plus, it sounded like there was a toilet paper shortage.

Stay home.

"Shit," Go-Go whispered. She collected a handful of granola bars from the pantry and six bottles of water from the fridge and crept back upstairs. Mrs. Johnson had finished her shower. She came out of the bathroom with a towel wrapped on her head, humming while rubbing one of her numerous creams on her face. Go-Go froze.

"Honey?" Mr. Johnson's voice called up the stairs. Mrs. Johnson didn't hear him. Go-Go ducked into the guest room. The attic entry was in the closet of the master.

Shit, shit, shit. She was stupid to come down like this. Dave should have come with her. They should have left. But she didn't know. How could she know?

"Honey, they're telling everyone to stay home." Mr. Johnson's voice said from the hallway.

"I have to go to work, though," Mrs. Johnson said.

"Check your email and see."

They both left the hallway. Go-Go took a risk and scurried to the master bedroom and into the closet. She closed the door just as Mrs. Johnson came back into the bedroom, muttering about working from home.

"Go?" Dave's voice above her. She handed up the snacks and he helped her up into the attic. She filled him in on what was going on.

"They're not leaving?" he asked, panic in his voice.

She shook her head.

Mr. Johnson set up his work-from-home space in the kitchen.

Mrs. Johnson set hers up at the dining room table.

After their food stores dissipated and their water supply vanished, Go-Go knew it was only a matter of days. They spent their time talking about how life would have been after Dave started working and they moved out of Bobby's place. How they'd buy their own home, maybe start a family. Go-Go didn't want kids though, so she said they'd rescue dogs. Four, maybe even five dogs.

"I'm sorry about this, Dave," Go-Go said. "You wanted to stop doing this more than once, but I got caught up in the thrill of it."

He didn't say anything. She turned and looked at him.

His eyes stared up at the eaves, glassy, glazed. His mouth hung open. He was gone.

Go-Go wept but she wanted to sob and bawl. She wanted to be noisy in her grief. But she didn't have the energy.

"What is that smell?" Margot Johnson wondered out loud standing in her walk-in closet. She worked from home now, sure, and she had gained quite a bit of weight with the kitchen so nearby her workspace, but she liked to look at her clothes. At the pantsuits she used to wear to the office. Her cute shoes. She'd been wearing the same stained gray sweatpants for two weeks straight.

Something dripped onto the carpet. She jumped back, startled. Then crouched and looked at it. It was white. It moved. Another one dropped next to it, then another. Something hit her head. Margot jumped back and shook out her hair. The white thing came away in her hand. More of them dropped from the ceiling.

She looked up and screamed.

The attic access was open a crack. Fingers in a frozen curl gripped the edge of the opening. Pressed into the crack, a cloudy eyeball peered from within a face shrouded with crawling white maggots.

Acknowledgments

Thank you so much for reading, *Tommy's Teeth and Other Tales*.

As I always say, a book cannot be written nor produced without the help of amazing supporters.

Thank you to the creator of The Storymatic prompt cards (six trillion stories in one little box), Brian Mooney. Without these amazing little cards, I would have had to use some other sub-par prompt generator, and let's face it, all others pale in comparison to The Storymatic.

Thank you to my newsletter subscribers, especially Robert the Demented and Joannie Sico. Thank you to Melba Farley for lending me her name for "Amelia's Monster," even though you are anything but.

Thank you to my biggest supporters, Melissa McMurphy, Amanda Keil, Jessa Forest (fellow horror author), and LS Hawker (fellow thriller author).

Thank you to Uluru. I grovel at thy feet as you bestow upon me thy blessings and creative wisdom.

Thank you to my family: my twin sister Wissa, my brother James, and my parents May and Barry Brouhard.

A big fat thank you to my editor, Proof Positive, for making sure I didn't make any silly typos, punctuation, or grammatical mistakes.

A huge thank you to my beloved pittie mix, Kira, for

her emotional support, cuddles, shenanigans (hey, Shanaynay), and pure joy.

And the biggest bucket of ~~blood and guts~~ gratitude for my husband, Tim. Your love, support, care, feeding, and making sure I get fresh air, sunlight, and time in nature keep me vibrantly alive. I love you.

About the Author

Claire L. Fishback lives in Morrison, Colorado with her loving husband, Tim, and their pit bull mix, Kira. Writing has been her passion since age six. When she isn't writing, she enjoys mountain biking, hiking, running, baking, and adding to her bone collection, though she would rather be stretched out on the couch with a good book (or poking dead things with sticks).

Please visit www.horrorandmore-er.com to sign up for a free eBook!